Coffee & Cases

S amuel Pepys speared a slice of brawn with his knife, bit off a chunk, and washed it down with a greedy slug of wine. "The King's favourite - Haut-Brion from Bordeaux," he noted with satisfaction, smacking his lips.

Seated opposite him across the oak dining table, Jacob Standish eyed the drink enviously as he supped his bitter, weak beer. "You have fine taste, sir," he said.

"Mmm," Pepys replied, nodding sagely.

The two men were taking breakfast at Pepys's home on Seething Lane, in the east of the city of London. An elegant red-brick building on three floors, it was provided for him by the Navy Board, whom he served as Clerk of the Acts. One of the highest positions attainable within King Charles II's navy - essentially its chief administrator - Pepys had settled comfortably into the position of power and status that afforded him.

Pepys, 33, had a clean-shaven, open face which, coupled with his innate joie de vivre, made him appear almost boyish at times. He was wearing white silk breeches, a billowing cotton shirt and a long, embroidered velvet waistcoat.

Jacob Standish, eleven years his junior, was his personal inquisitor, charged with investigating any wrong-doing that befell him or, should Pepys see fit, his friends, colleagues and relatives. Pepys had taken him on as a favour to his late colleague, Surveyor to the Navy Board, Sir Miles Standish, the young man's father. His first impressions had not been savoury; Jacob appeared clumsy and hesitant, with overgrown eyebrows that met in the middle.

Yet already, in little over a fortnight, the fledgling inquisitor was proving Pepys wrong. Jacob, it turned out, had a keen eye for detail and an enquiring mind, as well as a tall, powerful build that he was not afraid to use in threatening circumstances. Only yesterday - being the 19th of September, 1666 - Jacob had returned from Deptford's royal dockyard, having helped to unmask a murderer in plague-doctor garb who had terrorised the area by night.

Sitting beside Jacob at the table was Abigail Harcourt, the young woman who had aided him in those endeavours. Formerly - until yesterday, in fact - Pepys's housemaid, her bravura performances and shrewd deductions had impressed her master so greatly that he had promoted her to the same role as Jacob.

Also by Ellis Blackwood

The Samuel Pepys Mysteries
Book 0.5: Mr Pepys's Stolen Diaries
(via ellisblackwood.com)
Book 1: The Brampton Witch Murders
Book 2: The Plague Doctor Murders
Book 3: The Coffee House Murders
Book 4: The King's Court Murders
Book 5: The Frost Fair Murders

Scan the QR code for social links and website.

The Coffee House Murders

The Samuel Pepys Mysteries Book 3

Ellis Blackwood

Vintage Mystery Press

ISBN: 978-1-0687027-2-3

Cover design, editorial & historical fact-checking: Tim Brown, A.S.C. (Rtd).

Cover illustration licensed from shutterstock.com.

For Dylan, my go-to Sichuan hotpot and cider companion.

Contents

Samuel Pepys now had two personal inquisitors. Only one of them looked comfortable at his dining table.

"Abigail, will you not sample the brawn?" Pepys asked, sampling some more himself. "It is most exquisite."

She sat awkwardly, her turquoise eyes unblinking, like a cornered hare in a lantern's glare. "Master Pepys, I've lit the fireplaces," she motioned towards the roaring hearth behind her, which was cutting through a distinct chill in the air, "but the linen concerns me. It…"

Pepys held up his hand, eyes closed. "Nay, Abigail, your prior duties here are now firmly in the past. If you are to be my personal inquisitor, you cannot be seen in public wearing a gown as delightful as yours that is sullied with soot."

Abby, 19 and petite, nodded, causing her long, flame-red hair, which she had not yet tied up, to slide over her shoulders. She pushed it back, her freckled cheeks reddening.

Why am I so tense? she wondered. *This new promotion is more than I could have dreamed of.*

She could think of no other man of standing in London – her master knew a few, who had been guests here, and whose chamber pots she had emptied – who would have been progressive enough, or brazen enough, to do as Master Pepys had done for her.

So why do I feel so stiff, seated at a meal table with these two men?

Then she realised: *deep down, I don't believe I deserve it.*
Abby shook herself.

Pepys noticed and asked, "Do you ail, Abigail?"

Before she could respond, Jacob, who had been inspecting an apple, spoke up. "Sir, I am keen to return to my own house, which I have not visited since we began our association on the night of the terrible fire that engulfed London. But I would first learn what plans you have for our next investigation." He paused. "If it pleases you?"

Pepys put down his knife and quaffed some more wine. "It pleases me greatly, Mr Standish! My inquisitors are the talk of the Navy Board, if not yet all of London, and I am eager to send you forth on your latest intrepid investigation."

Feeling a tingle at the nape of her neck, Abby perked up.

Pepys rested his hands on the linen tablecloth. Although he had washed his hands in water not an hour ago, he noticed his fingernails were already dirty. Clearing his throat, he announced, "I have lost my brass pocket watch."

Jacob felt his broad shoulders slump and turned to Abby, who avoided his gaze. He could sense that she was frowning.

"Your pocket watch, sir," said Jacob. "Is lost?" He had confronted Deptford's murderous Plague Doctor and prior to that had saved Pepys's sister from the hangman's noose, when she was accused of witchcraft. "Might it have been stolen?" he asked hopefully.

Pepys thought for a moment. "I consider it unlikely," he replied. "But, aye, it may be so."

Jacob exhaled deeply. "The Lord be praised!"

Before his mentor could respond, Abby butted in, "I believe what Jacob was trying to say is…" She knew precisely what Jacob was saying - that, given their new-found experience, investigating a pocket watch that had merely been misplaced was beneath them - but could not figure out how to reword it.

So they sat there, Pepys eyeing each inquisitor in turn expectantly with his bright, bulging brown eyes.

Jacob broke the silence. "Where was this watch stolen… or indeed lost? Mr Pepys?"

"A fine question," replied Pepys. "Your prowess as an inquisitor grows with each passing day, Mr Standish."

Abby lofted an eyebrow.

"It was lost, or indeed stolen, at the western end of The Strand. At Charing Cross," Pepys explained. "When I did visit a coffee house there, the name of which escapes me."

Abby lowered her head. "Sir, if you remember, I once accompanied you to a coffee house, in your service, and was barred entry."

Pepys nodded. "I remember it well, Abigail. Mr Farr's establishment on Fleet Street. The Rainbow. Frequented by freemasons and French Huguenots, such as my dear wife, Elizabeth, is descended from."

"How is your wife, sir?" Jacob asked.

"Another fine question," Abby muttered under her breath.

"Alas, she has a touch of the vapours and is confined to her chamber," Pepys replied.

"Can I assist the mistress?" Abby asked.

"Nay, Abigail. She is well attended. Your attention as my personal inquisitor lies in returning to me my watch…"

"But, sir, women are denied entry to coffee houses, which would…"

Pepys hushed her with a gesture. "Fear not. The proprietor of this coffee house on The Strand, in which I misplaced my watch – or perhaps in which it was stolen – was of the fairer sex. I am confident she will welcome your patronage."

The talk at the table turned to coffee. Abby had managed to sample the fashionable new drink during the inquisitors' previous investigation in Deptford, and had found it too bitter for her liking – though she had enjoyed the sweetness of the added sugar. Jacob, likewise, was no enthusiast, however he did not let on for fear of appearing uncouth.

Pepys, on the other hand, pronounced himself a connoisseur of the brew. He had visited London's first coffee house, he informed Abby and Jacob proudly, "Which was opened in 1652 by an enterprising merchant named Daniel Edwards."

Edwards, he went on to explain, had acquired a taste for the drink while on business in Turkey. On returning to London, he brought with him a Greek man by the name of Pasqua Rosée, who was well versed in the ritual of coffee-making.

Noticing that his friends always seemed to turn up when the aroma of the roasting coffee began wafting from his windows, Edwards spotted an opportunity to make money. He set Pasqua up in a shed in the churchyard of St Michael's, Cornhill, conveniently close to the Royal Exchange shopping arcade, where merchants gathered.

"Hold!" Pepys exclaimed suddenly and bustled upstairs to his study.

When he returned, he placed a small, rather rumpled sheet of paper on the table before his inquisitors. "I secured this keepsake," he said. "Pasqua's own handbill, titled 'The Vertue of the Coffee Drink'."

It began:

The Grain or Berry called Coffee, groweth upon little Trees, only in the Deserts of Arabia.

It is brought from thence, and drunk generally throughout all the Grand Seigniors Dominions.

Having explained the process of brewing, Pasqua's handbill went on to make a series of claims for coffee's health benefits:

It supresseth Fumes exceedingly, and therefore good against the Head-ach, and will very much stop any Defluxion of Rheumas, that distil from the Head upon the Stomach, and so prevent and help the Consumptions and the Cough of the Lungs.

It is excellent to prevent and cure the Dropsy, Gout, and Scurvy.

It is known by experience to be better then any other Drying Drink for People in years, or Children that have any running humors upon them, as the Kings Evil. &c.

It is very good to prevent Mis-carryings in Child-bearing Women.

It is a most excellent Remedy against the Spleen, Hypocondriack Winds, or the like.

Warning against drinking coffee after supper, since it "prevents drowsiness" and will "hinder sleep for 3 or 4 hours", the text concluded:

It is neither Laxative nor Restringent.

Made and Sold in St. Michaels Alley in Cornhill, by Pasqua Rosee, at the Signe of his own Head.

"Curious fellow," said Jacob. "Does he still reside in London?"

Pepys shrugged. "No man knows what became of him. Rumour has it that he left the city following some misdemeanour, to open a coffee house abroad."

Abby pushed the handbill back towards Pepys. "Sir, we haven't yet asked about your watch. How, pray, did you come to misplace it?"

Pepys explained that he had been walking along The Strand towards Whitehall Palace a few days ago. He was heading to a meeting with the King, concerning the aftermath of the fire, when he was accosted by a man who was well-dressed, "if somewhat ill-scented." After introducing himself, this strange fellow assured Pepys they had been acquainted and asked him what time it was. Subsequently, he had admired Pepys's new brass pocket watch.

"I recall our discourse, since the watch thereafter disappeared," said Pepys.

"This man stole it?" Jacob asked.

"Nay, Mr Standish, for I had the watch on my person when I later attended the coffee house."

Some way further along The Strand, Pepys said, he was accosted by another man who was also smartly attired, wearing a blue jewelled brooch that caught his eye. This second fellow claimed to know him, even recalled visiting him at Seething Lane, although Pepys had no memory of such a visit, nor of the man himself.

"He invited me to sup coffee with him," he said, "that we might exchange the latest tidings."

Abby interjected, "And you agreed?"

Pepys regarded her askance. "I did not wish to offend the fellow, who had assured me we were acquainted!"

"Indeed. Pray continue, Master Pepys," Abby replied, the faintest of smiles on her lips.

"There is little more to tell. I did accompany him to the coffee house near Charing Cross, the name of which I forget, and ere I departed, I discovered that my watch was missing."

"What was the nature of your discourse with this man, sir? Did he remark upon the watch?"

"Nay, Mr Standish. He did not mention it." Pepys paused, clearly unsure whether to continue.

"Is there aught else?" asked Jacob.

Pepys harrumphed. "He was adamant that I play cards with him," he replied at length.

"To gamble, sir?"

"Aye, Mr Standish," Pepys replied, grimacing at the memory. "A man of my standing! I did rebuke him forcefully, sir, and he duly cowered, begging my pardon, ere he bade his leave with great solemnity."

Abby spoke up. "And you discovered the watch was missing only after you left the coffee house?"

Pepys nodded and produced from inside his waistcoat a linen pouch on a length of cord, which was hung over his shoulder. "I kept it here. As I continued along King Street to my meeting with His Majesty, fearing that my delay may have rendered me tardy, I checked this pocket and discovered it to be empty."

"You consider that the watch was misplaced, rather than stolen?" Jacob pressed him.

Pepys pulled himself upright. "I consider, sir, that no common thief could outwit Samuel Pepys."

"What manner of clientele frequented this coffee house, Master Pepys?" Abby asked.

Pepys wrinkled his nose. "A loathsome bunch of fellows, Abigail, much entertained by the sound of their own voices. 'Twas a coffee house, I believe, that was frequented by wits."

Chapter Two

To Strand Lane

On their way by water to Westminster, the inquisitors were forced to endure another sight of London's destruction. Having viewed the ruins only briefly before setting off for Deptford, they were now presented with the full vista of the desolate city.

They were rowed upriver not by Pepys's usual rivermen, the Kilgore brothers, but by a glum-faced pair who pulled at their oars with their hat-brims tugged down low. Jacob, who had found Clement Kilgore, in particular, to be an impudent cove, was quietly relieved. The mood aboard the little wherry was sombre.

Some four-fifths of the city had been levelled - from the street beyond Seething Lane in the east, as far north as the ancient wall, and west into Westminster. *How miraculous it is that my mentor's house escaped the flames,* Jacob marvelled.

The great swathe of rubble still smoked and smouldered, with isolated fires still burning more than a fortnight after the conflagration began. People moved among the ruins, and a handful of makeshift hovels had been constructed - owners, the inquisitors assumed, staking claim to their land.

Most glaringly absent was the edifice that, until so recently, had dominated the London skyline: the cathedral of St Paul's. Though its spire had been destroyed by an earlier fire, the remaining tower still dwarfed all around it. Unlike the surrounding properties, made chiefly of wood, St Paul's had been built of stone. Yet it, too, was gone.

The wirier of their two rivermen must have noticed the inquisitors staring, appalled, in the direction of St Paul's, for he spoke up without warning. "So fearsome was the heat, the very stonework was rended. Even the great bells melted to but a vapour." Then he fell silent again, his dread words hanging in the river's rotten air.

Only once they had passed the River Fleet and Whitefriars did London begin to reappear. The sudden, unexpected sight of tall buildings, and of gardens and fields beyond, felt like godly intervention.

As their wherry drifted towards the wooden landing steps at the bottom of Strand Lane, Abby gazed back downriver at the many hundreds of variously sized craft jostling for space. On the faces aboard that she could make out, few looked to be taking in the fearful scene the way she just had. Instead, their attentions were elsewhere:

on one another, or on some more pressing matter in hand.

Londoners, she assured herself, were reacquainting themselves with their daily lives. It was what London folk did, and such stoicism made her feel proud.

Jacob had pleaded with Abby to stop off at his house on Strand Lane, for a change of attire and to check for fire damage. In truth, she had not needed much persuasion, given the apparent lack of urgency of their latest investigation (and indeed their enthusiasm for it).

Disembarking, they found Somerset House to their left and Arundel House to their right - both vast, imposing properties set back behind sprawling ornamental gardens arranged in geometric patterns. There were trees - actual surviving trees - beside them, covered in leaves bearing the golden hues of early autumn. Both inquisitors found themselves breathing in the air, savouring nature's resilience.

"Where's your house?" Abby asked, eager to see where Jacob lived.

"At the top of the lane," he replied, setting off up the sloping street.

Hoisting the hem of her gown, she hurried after him.

After a dog-leg, Strand Lane ended where it met The Strand, which ran perpendicular. In every direction, the buildings were undamaged. There was a sense of space on this eastern edge of Westminster, which had none of the narrow alleyways and clustered housing of the city. The air would no doubt have smelled cleaner, were it not for the acrid fumes drifting in from the smouldering ruins of the city.

This was where the rich folk lived.

And in amongst them, Jacob.

The inquisitor was hunting in his satchel for a key, stood before the elegant door of a red-brick townhouse, not dissimilar to Mr Pepys's. It too was set on three floors, flat-fronted not jettied, with large, leaded bay windows.

Abby gazed up at the gabled roof and whistled. "You live here by yourself?"

"Aye," he replied, unlocking the door and entering. "There was a maidservant, but I dismissed her."

"Why?" Abby asked.

When Jacob failed to reply, she followed him into a dingy, panelled hallway.

Abby noticed two doors on either side and a staircase leading off to the left. Then the front door closed behind them, and she was engulfed in darkness.

The space smelled of smoke, which must have infiltrated the property through every tiny gap in its exterior.

She heard Jacob's movement, feeling his way around the walls, until he let out a yelp and began, as far as she could tell, hopping around on one foot.

"Had I used the doorstop to prop open the door," she heard him mutter to himself, "then perchance I would not have stubbed my toe upon it."

Abby felt for the nearest door handle, found it easily, and opened the door.

"The parlour," Jacob explained behind her.

Guided by a thin shaft of light, Abby made for the window shutters and pushed open one side, then the other, flooding the room with daylight. She opened the window to allow air in, hoping the smell of smoke would travel in the opposite direction.

When she turned around, Jacob was right in front of her, causing her to jump.

"I do beg your pardon," he said, backing away. "The parlour."

"Aye, you said." She noticed he was fiddling with his periwig.

The room had a high, plastered ceiling and was panelled in dark wood - not that a great deal of pan-elling was evident, so numerous were the gilt-framed paintings around the walls. Above an imposing stone fireplace - the focus of any visitor's attention - was the family coat of arms: a blue-and-red shield emblazoned with an anchor, two crossed swords and a phoenix, supported by a rearing lion and griffin. Underneath was the Latin motto, "Ex Umbra in Veritatem", which meant nothing to Abby.

To the right of the crest was a portrait of a gentleman wearing a curly, chestnut periwig that flowed below his shoulders. He wore a billowing, embroidered, royal blue cloak with a wide lace collar. Clean-shaven with silver eyebrows, he had an inscrutable look and vivid blue, glinting eyes.

"Your father, Sir Miles?" she asked, although she already knew the answer.

To Abby, he looked like the sort of man who might teach Latin rather than hold a position of authority in the mighty King's navy.

"Aye," Jacob replied, clearing a lump from his throat.

She was wondering where Jacob got his distinctive looks, until her eyes were drawn to a smaller - if still outsized - portrait of a middle-aged lady wearing a luxurious silk gown in rich orange with silvery-blue satin sleeves. Several strings of pearls adorned her neck, and though wispy brown curls framed her face, they did little to soften her stern, haughty expression. Her thick-set eyebrows met in the middle.

"You rarely speak of your mother," Abby pointed out.

"Indeed," Jacob replied. "We have not spoken since my father's funeral."

"She resides at Standish Hall in Woolwich?"

Jacob nodded.

"Then why not visit her there?"

"She requested that I not do so."

Abby glanced at Jacob. He was staring up at the same portrait, pinching his lower lip.

Abby had a plan, she told Jacob, which required him to dress in one of his finest outfits.

He looked down at his baggy-kneed breeches and old leather shoes. A hole in one of the soles had allowed a dirty-water stain to creep up his white stocking. "I could not promise that I possess such a thing," he said.

She stood before him, attempting to brush something soggy off his collar, her eyeline level with his chest. "Could you not borrow from your father's wardrobe?"

Swiping her hand away, he snapped, "I would not dream of it!"

She gasped. "I'm sorry if I…"

As quickly as his anger had appeared, it was gone. Jacob's shoulders slumped and he sighed. "My father was ten times - nay a hundred times - the man I am. I am not worthy to wear his clothes."

She took his hand and looked up at him; he would not meet her gaze. "I didn't know your father, Jacob, and I'm sure he was a fine and admirable gentleman." She squeezed gently. "But I do know you, and I truly believe you are worthy of wearing any man's clothes."

When his hazel eyes met hers, she swore they glistened with unshed tears.

"I suppose I am only borrowing them," he said quietly.

As the sound of his heavy footsteps faded up a wooden staircase, Abby was left alone in the parlour. She busied herself with opening the remaining shutters before instinctively building a fire in the hearth. *Force of habit*, she thought to herself.

Even when it was lit, the room still felt cold.

When Jacob returned, Abby was sitting in a richly upholstered armchair that dwarfed her dainty frame. She was warming her stockinged feet at the fire.

On seeing him, she clapped her hands. "You look like a gentleman!" she exclaimed, heartened to see the hint of a smile on his face.

"I managed to find several items of attire the maid had laundered," he told her. "'Tis a shame I dismissed her."

"Why did you dismiss her?"

Jacob shrugged. "I did not feel that I was worthy of servants."

Abby let it go. Gesturing around the room, she asked, "Who are all the people in these portraits?"

"Members of the Standish family."

"Yet I don't see you here?"

Jacob slumped onto a chaise longue. Resting his elbows in his lap, he bowed his head.

Although he's wearing that old bird's-nest of a periwig, his black velvet coat with brass buttons, lately pressed shirt and lace sleeves make him look rather dashing, she thought.

She rose and crossed to him, knelt and took his hands in hers. He did not resist.

"Families can be a blessing and a curse," she said quietly. She hoped that he would meet her gaze, but his head remained bowed.

Jacob sniffed. "Some more than others," he mumbled.

"You don't need to tell me, Jacob."

"Aye. I would prefer not to."

Silence.

Abby stroked the back of his hand with her thumb. "Then perhaps the gist?"

To her surprise, Jacob burst out laughing. As he did so, some colour returned to his drawn features. "You were born to be an inquisitor, Abigail Harcourt," he told her.

Jacob gave Abby a tour of the parlour's portraiture, awkwardly at first, but increasingly softly spoken when they reached his siblings.

The three demure young women displayed side by side at the end of the room, he explained, were his sisters, Elizabeth, Margaret and Anne. Each was rosy-cheeked and pert of nose.

"Where are they now?" Abby asked him.

"Elizabeth married a wealthy merchant in Bristol. Margaret wed the Earl of Norfolk. Anne, the youngest, is a courtier."

"Your sister is *one of the King's courtiers!*"

Anne was indeed a beautiful young woman, with loose blonde curls, her father's blue eyes, and a mischievous smile. None of the girls had inherited their mother's eyebrows.

That honour went to the male bloodline. "Those must be your brothers?" Abby said as they reached a pair of portraits depicting earnest young men in blue doublets with red sashes, clutching hourglasses, who looked remarkably similar. "Are they twins?"

"Aye," Jacob replied, almost mumbling. "They were. They died in the service of the King."

Abby pictured his family in her mind: *two dead, heroic brothers, two successfully married sisters, another sister installed in Whitehall Palace beside - very close beside - King Charles himself, and a mother who shunned him…*

She realised she had pushed Jacob as far as she dared. "I beg your pardon," she said softly. "I did not mean to intrude."

Something inside him snapped. He ripped off his periwig and hurled it across the room, knocking one of a pair of porcelain vases off a table. It smashed to smithereens on the wooden floor. "But you did intrude, Abigail!" he exclaimed, storming toward the door. "You did intrude!" he repeated, his voice more anguished than angered, and slammed the door behind him.

"My siblings are all dead," she called after him.

Chapter Three

The Coney-Catchers Pt I

Abby thought it best to leave Jacob alone with his musings. She debated nosing around the house, but thought better of it, and contented herself with investigating the kitchen for nourishment.

She found none.

The modestly sized, stone-tiled room was pristine, as if it had not been used since the maid last cleaned. The copper pots and pans, the crockery, the work surfaces - all spotless. The pantry was empty, save for one small sack of flour, and while the spice jars were full, there were no ingredients to flavour. Even the brickwork of the hearth looked freshly scrubbed.

At the back of a cupboard, Abby found a jar of preserved apricots, and greedily pawed the contents into her mouth. She could find nothing to drink, not even a musty old bottle of wine, and realised she was very thirsty.

When finally Jacob appeared, striding into the parlour where Abby was waiting - she had cleaned up the broken pottery - he picked up his periwig, centred it on his head, and topped it off with a shapely feathered hat. "Shall we depart?" he asked, as if nothing untoward had occurred.

Dusk was falling as they emerged onto The Strand. A church bell chimed its first of seven, and Abby looked to her right to follow the sound.

"St Clement Danes," Jacob said, without looking.

The tiered tower of the church stood like a sentinel at the eastern end of The Strand. Its pale stone was barely visible beneath layers of soot.

A second bell, much nearer, then began to chime, and Abby noticed they were in the lee of another church, strikingly similar architecturally to the other.

"St Mary-le-Strand," said Jacob. "The bells keep me awake at night."

Abby knew Westminster, having run errands for Pepys there in the past. She marvelled at the width of the roads. Up ahead, two yellow-painted hackney coaches, each drawn by two horses, passed one another with ease, heading in opposite directions. In the city there were lanes a single coach could barely navigate.

Lined up near St Mary-le-Strand was a row of waiting hackney coaches, beneath a tall maypole. The drivers were idly smoking pipes and tinkering with their vehicles.

"We too could hire a coach," suggested Jacob.

"Nay," Abby told him. "It is vital that we walk."

He squinted at her, shaking his head, but was already learning not to question her wisdom.

The Strand was the most impressive street Abby had ever seen. Its houses were built of fine red-brown brick—none of the timber and plaster that had fuelled the recent fire in the city—with tall glass windows and classical columns. Rainwater, when it came, was directed into the paved street by neat guttering. Stranger still to her, many neighbouring houses were of uniform height and design, almost resembling palaces.

At ground level were the commercial delights - many shops (now closed for the day), sufficient taverns and a smattering of coffee houses - and there were plenty of people about, having lately finished their work. Candles and oil lamps burned in windows, creating a golden glow under the blue-black sky.

As they neared the venerable Savoy Hospital for the poor, Abby asked, "How long until we reach Charing Cross?"

"Ten minutes?" he suggested.

"I expected our quarry to have appeared by now," Abby said. "You should walk ahead of me, Jacob." (Which was not difficult, Jacob's strides being twice the length of hers.)

Gratefully, Abby allowed herself to slow down. She watched as her fellow inquisitor continued up The Strand in his familiar loping gait.

It was not long before she spotted a man loitering in the shelter of a grand doorway, on the opposite side of the street. His garb appeared foppish and ostentatious.

Most Londoners were in a hurry, but not this one. He was watching Jacob.

Then, the door behind him opened, a servant appeared and shooed him away. Instead of disappearing up the road, he crossed it, walking in Jacob's direction.

Abby had fallen a little too far behind and quickened her pace.

Aye! she thought as the man halted Jacob, bowed briefly, and the two men fell into conversation.

When she was twenty yards behind them, she stopped and pressed herself into the shadows.

Is Jacob laughing? she wondered, as her fellow inquisitor clutched at his sides and bent double.

A minute or two later, the other man held Jacob by the shoulders, as if they were long-lost friends, then drew back and bowed. When Jacob returned the gesture, the other man crossed the road with a cheery wave. As she watched, he walked casually past her on the other side, heading in the direction of St Mary-le-Strand.

She ran to catch up with Jacob.

"What a charming fellow!" he exclaimed.

"Who was he?"

"Claimed he swore he knew me, but could not place it. When I informed him that I was Jacob Standish, son of the late Sir Miles Standish, residing on Strand Lane, his entire face illuminated, and he knew me straight away."

"How marvellous," Abby replied, rather more deadpan than he might have expected.

"Then, of course, I remembered him."

"Who was he?"

"His name escapes me now. But a true gentleman. *Did you witness his attire?* He requested that I accompany him to a tavern, that we might share bawdy tales of the old days." Jacob lofted a finger, grinning. "But I told him, 'Nay, sir. I have urgent business elsewhere.'" Pausing, he added wistfully, "I shall miss him."

"Excellent," said Abby. "I have an errand to run. I'll meet you in the coffee house at the end of The Strand, by Charing Cross."

Before he could reply, she was gone, racing off towards St Mary-le-Strand.

Chapter Four

The Coney-Catchers Pt II

J acob reached the fashionable New Exchange shopping arcade and looked for Abby. She was nowhere to be seen.

The New Exchange was a truly impressive structure, Gothic-styled, with two long arched galleries set atop one another. Charles I, he recalled being told, had attended its grand opening as a boy. Inside, merchants and shopkeepers catered to the hearts' desires of the well-off, selling everything from clothing and millinery to furniture and books. Women favoured the establishment. Jacob had never much cared for the business of shopping.

He crossed the street, aware that The Strand was coming to an end, and would soon fork at Charing Cross to become Cockspur Street (a main route towards Reading and the south-west) and King Street, which led towards Whitehall and the King's court.

On the corner of The Strand and St Martin's Lane, he stopped. *I have reached my destination*, he thought to himself. *Yet nought amiss has occurred? And where is this coffee house with its female proprietor?* There was no such establishment in evidence, only a row of shops.

Jacob looked again for Abby but saw only strangers.

When he turned back, there was a man standing in front of him. The gentleman appeared middle-aged, and sported a long, embroidered, rich-green tunic with a silk waistcoat beneath. A satin scarf was tucked around his neck, and his periwig was one of the longest Jacob had seen, reaching down almost below the man's chest. Truly, this was a gentleman of means... and yet, his face was scarred and chapped. *Did he serve in a war?* Jacob wondered.

"Do I know you, sir?" the man asked, in a tone suggesting he did.

Jacob eyed him curiously. "I do not believe..."

"Mr Jacob Standish!" the man interjected. "Of Strand Lane, if I am not greatly mistaken?"

Jacob wracked his brain to recall the other man's face, for fear of causing offence.

As if reading Jacob's mind, his new friend introduced himself. "Sir James Quigley," he said with a bow, which Jacob returned. "I am a friend of your cousin, George, sir. If you recall, we became acquainted at one of his celebrations. In honour of the King."

In honour of the King! thought Jacob.

However, he did not recall the celebration. Indeed, he had no recollection of any such cousin, although the Standish family tendrils were widespread indeed. "Aye!" he replied, laughing unnecessarily. "I remember it well, sir! How is Cousin Geoffrey?"

"George, sir."

"I beg your pardon. Cousin George."

Quigley's face fell. "I fear he died, sir."

"Died?" Jacob replied, instantly sapped of mirth.

"Aye, good sir. Pray, accept my profound sympathies."

Jacob found himself at a loss, mourning the passing of a man he had never known, yet felt certain must have lived, since Sir James Quigley had told him so. Bowing his head respectfully, he enquired, "How did he die, sir?"

Quigley blinked. "How did he die?"

"Aye, sir. What was the cause of my cousin's tragic demise?"

"Why, he…" Sir James dipped inside his coat and produced a small silver box, from which he inhaled a pinch of snuff. "He fell from a bridge."

"*He fell from a bridge?* How, sir? Was he drunk?"

Quigley took Jacob by the arm. "I appreciate this is lamentable news, Mr Standish. What say you we continue our discourse in this coffee house?" he asked, pointing to a battered old door beside a shuttered shop window. "The brew will warm our spirits on this sorrowful occasion."

It was only then that Jacob noticed the sign above the door, hanging from an iron bracket. Weather-beaten, cracked and faded, he could just make out the words:

ROSE'S
COFFEE
HOUSE

Except that the sign appeared so old and damaged, it read more like:

ROSE'S
COFEE
HOSE

"Are we buying coffee, Sir James, or stockings?" Jacob quipped.

Quigley did not dignify the remark, but opened the door and bade the inquisitor enter.

A steep set of stairs led down into a dingy stairwell, illuminated by a single candle. There was a door at the bottom.

This coffee house is in a basement, Jacob thought to himself. *No wonder I could not see it from the street.*

Quigley knocked twice on the lower door with his knuckle, and Jacob noticed for the first time that he wore gold and silver rings on each finger.

Shortly, a bolt was pulled back on the other side of the door, and it opened. A woman stood, raising an eyebrow at the pair of them. Her hair was jet black, pulled back and gathered in a bun at the nape of her neck, and her eyes were warm and golden. A simple lace cap covered her head, tied with a ribbon under her chin.

She was dressed in a red gown over layered petticoats, gathered at the waist by a black belt with a silver buckle. Jacob estimated her to be in her late forties, although she could have been older. *Elegance disguises age well*, he thought to himself.

There was something about her expression - haughty, confident, and entirely out of place on a lady's face. Jacob swallowed dryly.

"Sir James," she said, stepping back to allow him through. "To what do we owe the honour?"

The inquisitor noticed her voice was a touch coarser than her elegant attire suggested.

Quigley motioned towards Jacob. "May I present a family acquaintance, Mr Jacob Standish? Of the Standish family of Greenwich."

She looked the inquisitor up and down, the hint of a smirk on her dry lips, while he was rooted to the spot in the stairwell. "Enter then, if you will!" she snapped. "I'm Rose," she added as he passed her. "This is my coffee house, and don't you forget it."

Jacob bowed awkwardly, grimacing.

Inside was a single, dreary room, barely larger than his kitchen (which was spacious). The walls were covered in notices, handbills, broadsides and pamphlets, some glued there, others tacked. Like all coffee houses, here was a space in which to discover news and the Arts.

A pall of tobacco smoke lingered among the low ceiling beams, and there was a fire in the hearth, over which a pot was suspended. Before the flames, two tall, curvy coffee pots were warming.

The smell of so much smoke in such a confined space ought to have sent Jacob fleeing for air; however, there was another, equally potent scent at work. That of roasting coffee. He had caught its allure the moment he entered.

There was room enough for just three tables. Only one was occupied, by three men wearing hats, periwigs and cravats, smoking long clay pipes. They appeared deep in a loud conversation and paid scant heed to the new arrivals.

At the far end were a battered wooden chest and a blanket-covered armchair. In front of the chair was a worktable, on top of which were jugs, a stack of ceramic dishes and wooden boxes, some opened, the largest brimming with raw green coffee beans. On the wall behind was a bookshelf piled with books and a set of empty wooden cubby-holes. At the end of the wall to the right was another door, leading, the inquisitor presumed, to the privy.

Jacob and Quigley pulled up a stool at one of the unoccupied tables and Rose set a small, handleless bowl in front of each of them. Then, wrapping a cloth around the handle, she lifted a coffee pot from the fire and filled Quigley's bowl.

As she moved the spout over Jacob's bowl, he put his hand in the way. "I… I cannot profess to enjoy the drink," he stammered.

"*Don't enjoy coffee?*" Rose exclaimed. "*Then what are you doing in a coffee house?*"

The three men at the other table began laughing uproariously, dabbing their noses with lace handkerchiefs.

"A man who does not enjoy coffee," the tallest one announced, "does not enjoy life!"

"I did wonder whether you served chocolate?" Jacob enquired meekly.

"Nay," Rose snapped, and began to pour, the inquisitor retracting his hand just in time to avoid a scalding.

"Who's paying?" she demanded, holding out an upturned palm.

Sir James looked expectantly towards Jacob.

Naturally, thought the inquisitor, *one could hardly expect a man of such standing to carry with him small change.*

"One penny each," stated Rose. "And tuppence more if you wish for a pipe of tobacco."

Quigley hurriedly accepted the offer; Jacob declined and pulled a coin pouch from his satchel. He did not notice the other man eyeing it covetously as he handed over the four pennies.

"Do you play cards, Mr Standish?" Quigley asked, sucking on his pipe.

"I fear I do not, sir," Jacob replied. He was no good with numbers, which tended to swim before his eyes. It was why he had failed as an apprentice naval purser, and why he avoided anything that involved counting, whenever possible.

Quigley unbuttoned his tunic, revealing a leather bag hung around his neck and a blue-jewelled brooch attached to his waistcoat. From the bag, he retrieved a box of playing cards.

Jacob looked puzzled. *Had not Mr Pepys mentioned a man wearing a jewelled brooch?*

As Quigley opened the box, there came several knocks on the door.

The three men at the other table instantly ceased their loud conversation and glanced anxiously towards the proprietor. Narrowing her eyes, she strode to the door, unbolted and opened it.

In stepped Abby.

The three men began jeering, to Abby's evident horror.

Rose silenced them with a glare. "Come in, my dear," she said. "Ignore the dullards. You are most welcome here."

The men appeared to enjoy her taunt enormously.

"Bravo!" said one, while the tallest stood and bowed deeply. "Eustace Dullard at your service, mistress!" he announced.

"Ignore the wits," Rose told Abby. "Their minds are smaller than the mice that run about their feet."

Which only set them off again.

Abby joined Jacob and Quigley at their table, addressing the latter. "I see you're playing cards, Mr...?"

Jacob butted in. "This gentleman is *Sir* James Quigley," he told her. "He is a good friend of my cousin Geoffrey."

"George," Quigley corrected him.

"Aye, Cousin George," Jacob affirmed.

"Is he, indeed?" said Abby, grinning at Quigley. "How marvellous. Do you enjoy gambling, Sir James? I had thought it was regulated in public places?"

Quigley glanced at Rose, who evil-eyed him back, and hastily he packed the cards back into their box. "A mere diversion!" he replied. "And you are, my dear?"

"Abigail Harcourt," she said. "This is my fellow inquisitor, Jacob Standish."

Jacob swore he saw the man turn ashen-faced. "Inquisitor, you say?"

"Aye," said Abby. "We investigate crime for Mr Samuel Pepys, who is Clerk of the Acts to the Navy Board. He advises the King himself."

Quigley had only taken in a small portion of her statement. "Investigate crime?"

"Aye, Sir James."

Sir James was buttoning up his coat, as if preparing to depart.

"Are you leaving?" Abby asked innocently. "I have only just arrived, and your coffee dish is but part-finished."

Quigley stood up. He seemed quite flustered. "Aye," he replied, "I have… There is…"

"Before you depart, might I trouble you for the time, sir?" she asked.

"Why, um, aye." Reaching inside his tunic, after some fumbling, he produced a large brass pocket watch. Jacob's jaw dropped.

"Such an exquisite timepiece, Sir James," said Abby. "May I see it?"

Before he could reply, she took it from his hand. It was indeed a lovely piece of work, with a brass surround, a single hour hand, and a scene of village life painted on an enamel centrepiece, surrounded by Roman numerals depicting the hours. Abby opened it up, revealing the intricate workings. "This is your watch?" she asked.

"Naturally," replied Quigley, trying to retrieve it.

"Then could you explain, perchance, why the name 'Samuel Pepys' is engraved here?"

"Sir James" had little choice but to come clean. His real name was Jim Quigley, he told them. Bluntly, he explained that he had a wife and six children to take care of, and that his duplicity and thieving kept them alive.

While Jacob wanted him arrested, Abby counselled caution. "Would you wish him hanged?" she asked, knowing that would be the inevitable outcome.

"Aye! I would!" Jacob replied. "The scoundrel had me believe my cousin had fallen to his death from a bridge!"

Abby had to stop herself from laughing. "Jim," she said to the other man, "you must know Westminster well?"

"Like the back of my hand."

"If we allow you your freedom, you will work for us," she told him. "That is the deal."

Jacob looked appalled.

"Then I accept it graciously," the old man replied, draining his coffee bowl and signalling for more.

"Why did we let him go?" Jacob asked in a high-pitched voice, after Quigley had finished his fourth coffee and left.

"Because, Jacob, he is a wily old criminal." She held up her hand as he was about to protest. "And it takes one to know one. He will make a useful ally."

"But…"

"If we are to investigate crimes in London, we shall need a network of informants like Jim Quigley."

Her words made sense – as they usually did – and Jacob found himself becoming convinced. "Are we able to trust him?"

"Only time will tell."

Jacob picked up Mr Pepys's watch from the table and inspected it. "For now, our latest investigation is closed," he said glumly. "What happened to that other man? The one you followed down The Strand?"

"Ah!" she exclaimed. "I almost forgot." Reaching into her satchel, she pulled out a gold locket on a chain. It was finely engraved with a family crest, and Jacob recognised it immediately.

Grabbing it from her, he opened the locket to find the tiny portrait of Sir Miles Standish. "My locket! Where…? How…?"

"The first coney-catcher," she said. "When he held you by the shoulders on The Strand, I saw him swipe it from your neck."

"Coney-catcher?" Jacob asked.

"You've not heard the term? A con-man and thief," she explained. "A coney is a tame rabbit bred for the pot."

Jacob thought for a moment. "Am I the tame rabbit?"

Abby laughed. "Nay, Jacob. But I suggest you heed lightly the words of men who crave power."

Chapter Five

Guy Kelburne

*A*nne Kelburne, wife of Henry Kelburne of Scotton in North Yorkshire, gave birth to her third son in the winter of 1607. They named the boy Guy after his uncle, as was the family tradition.

King James I was on the throne, far away in London - so far to the Kelburnes that he might as well have been on the moon. Although England's last war, against the Spanish, was but a memory, tensions throughout the kingdom were rising.

The King, an Anglican, had promised concessions to the Catholics, which had never materialised. Indeed, those of the old faith claimed to encounter only persecution.

An uneasy religious power struggle reigned in the country, in which the King held the upper hand.

Henry Kelburne was a miller, while Anne ran a smallholding and alehouse from their two-storey stone cottage in the harsh countryside, where crops were prone to fail and livestock was too often malnourished. Their four children, the eldest aged twelve, slept on straw upstairs, beneath a threadbare woollen blanket.

They were placid, God-fearing folk. Every Sunday, the family made the three-mile round trip to the nearest church, St Oswald's in Farnham – where Anne and Henry were married – with the father leading the horse-and-cart. Even at a young age, Guy sensed a tension in these journeys.

By and large, though, he was blissfully unaware of the poverty his family endured. To his eyes, every new corner was a discovery, rife with potential.

He loved to wander into his father's mill and climb among the grain sacks or draw shapes on the dusty floor. Henry had to keep a watchful eye on the child, who was apt to clamber over his machinery with no care for the hazards of the rotating wooden cogs and massive grinding stones.

Most of all, Guy enjoyed mingling with his mother's customers when the alehouse was open. They were farmers, blacksmiths and thatchers – men with calloused hands and colourful tales – who sat him on their knees while they supped, smoked and bantered.

To Anne's quiet consternation, her youngest son's favourite local was a heavily built master carpenter named George Lund, whose favourite tipple was Anne's cock ale.

Although the recipe – essentially a boiled chicken added to spiced ale and sack, stored for a good month before drinking – called for expensive ingredients, the profits were healthy, and the uncommon tipple made Anne's a destination hostelry. Men had been known to walk for miles just to sample the heady brew.

She would allow Guy to help her make a fresh batch, mashing the raisins, nutmeg, mace and dates, then adding them to the barrel. When George Lund first sampled a pot, he would ask the boy, "Did you make this, young Guy?" And the boy would nod eagerly.

George had the readiest laugh and the largest appetite, but also the quickest temper. He was known for speaking his mind and for his intransigence. He was all cheer at the beginning of an evening, but as the night wore on his belligerence grew, and he would often have to be placated, lest there be fisticuffs.

He was known as a man who could quarrel with his own shadow.

As Guy grew older, he began to notice such things.

Particularly tense were the nights when religion became the focus of the conversation. His father, when he was present, would wander outside seeking some convenient diversion whenever the words 'Anglican' and 'Catholic' were mentioned in the same heated breath.

His mother would glance around nervously, often eyeing the door, and when George became involved, she would threaten to take his ale from him (which usually did the trick). "Such discourse is forbidden in this house," she would tell him.

It was during one such altercation that Guy first heard the word 'recusant'.

George had recently been fined £20, he said – "my year's wages" – for not attending Anglican service at St Oswald's, and was forced to sell his horse to pay it. As his tale continued and the alcohol flowed, he grew increasingly irate. Friends slapped his back heartily and offered to buy him another drink, which Anne discreetly refused to serve, and the subject of conversation was changed. But George kept drifting back to it.

Eventually, Anne called for her husband and ordered him to eject the troublemaker. The master carpenter rose menacingly to his feet, fists at the ready, dwarfing the timid miller. "Let him stay, Anne," Guy heard his father mumble apologetically. "He's causing no harm."

That did it. She flew at George, pounding her fists on his barrel chest, and ordered him to leave her alehouse. Taken aback by such a fevered display from the usually placid woman, George held out his arms to fend off the blows.

Seeing his good friend so subdued, Guy joined the fray. "Leave him be!" he cried shrilly. "Leave him be!"

In the heat of the moment, Anne swatted her son aside. He fell into a table and lay on the floor in a daze, as tears welled under his eyelids.

Time stood still.

George rose to his full height. A look crossed his face that Anne had never seen before, and she backed away. "You mind yourself, George Lund," she told him. "Don't want to get yourself barred."

George folded his arms. "Why don't you tell him?" he said.

Tell me what? thought Guy. *When he looked around, he saw that the half-dozen other customers present were studiously inspecting their ales.*

"Tell him what?" *Anne replied with more fear than defiance.*

"You know."

She shook her head, on the verge of tears herself. "Nay, George," *she said quietly.*

The carpenter turned to Guy. "You know who your uncle is?" *he asked.* "The man with whose name you were christened?"

No one had told Guy that he had an uncle - or any relatives outside of their little household - let alone that he had been named after one. Pushing himself to his feet and pursing his lips defiantly, he shook his head.

"'Tis not your business, George Lund! We do not speak of family within this house!" *his mother exclaimed, then added in a resigned tone,* "No good will come of it."

"Let the boy decide," *George told her firmly.* "Guy, your uncle was Guy Fawkes."

The name meant nothing to him.

Chapter Six

A Royal Challenge

I n no great haste to return Mr Pepys's watch to him, Abby and Jacob perused the printed and handwritten papers spread around the walls of Rose's Coffee House. All manner of information was there, from the riveting to the nonsensical.

Noting their curiosity, Rose told them, "'Tis why London's coffee houses are known as 'Penny Universities'. You pay a penny for my wholesome, invigorating coffee, and with the same coin you may gain an education from the handbills and broadsides on my walls."

Eustace took to the floor. "A man would learn more in one hour in my company," he announced, "than he would in a year in any coffee house."

As he returned to his seat he was jeered by his companions.

The titles of the publications around the walls were often long-winded, and illustrated with woodcuts. Among them, Jacob spotted 'The Delights of the Bottle: Or the

Town Gallants' Declaration for Women and Wine'; 'A Most Certain, Strange, and True Discovery of a Witch' (which took Jacob's mind back to their recent investigation in Brampton); and 'Time's Precious Jewel, Or a Dialogue Between a Young-Man and Death, Being A Seasonable Warning for Youth to Forsake their Sins, and to lead a Religious Life Lest Death Surprise them and Repentance comes too late' (which made his head spin).

On the opposite wall, he found a cluster of broadside ballads: ''Tis a Plain Case Gentlemen', ''Tis Money Makes a Man: Or The Good-Fellow's Folly', 'Cromwell's Panegyrick'... Puzzled, he began to read the words:

Shall Presbyterian bells ring Cromwels praise,
While we stand still and do no Trophies raise
Until his lasting name? Then may we be
Hung like the bells in our dependencie.

The ballad went on for a good hundred more lines, and the point of the author's words eluded him. He made a mental note never again to concern himself with the meaning of the word 'panegyrick'.

He came across advertisements for quack medicines, alleged to cure every conceivable ailment, and noted that the peddler of many of these was one Zebulon Strangeway. *A most curious name*, he thought to himself.

As Jacob lingered over one handbill that looked freshly printed, he felt a presence behind him. It was the tallest of the wits, reading over his shoulder.

"Will you accept?" asked the wit.

Jacob swivelled his head. "Accept what, sir?"

"Why, the King's Challenge!" he replied, stabbing a long, bony finger at the title of the handbill: 'His Majesty's Royal Challenge of Wit and Eloquence'.

The man's breath reeked of coffee, tobacco and worse, and Jacob turned away. Hastily, he scanned the rest of the handbill.

An Exalted Competition of The Arts
Under the Auspices of His Royal Majesty King Charles
II, and the Esteemed Sponsorship of Jasper Davenport and
Clement Culpepper, Members of Parliament, all learned
Men of Letters are hereby invited to participate in a grand
Competition of The Arts, celebrating the Virtues of poetic
and prosaic expression.

Subject of the Competition.
Rebirth, Resilience, and The Royal Vision.
Submissions may take the form of essays, posies, or dra-
matic pieces, contemplating the future of our Illustrious
Kingdom, the Resilience of its People and the Benevolence
of the King.

The Prize.

50 Guineas and a private audience with His Majesty.

The Grand Reveal
Banqueting House, Whitehall.
At eleven of the clock on the morning of
Monday, Septemb. 24. 1666.

Jacob was no wit, he feared. "I shall not," he said.

"Most wise, sir!" replied the man. "For it would have been a woeful and senseless waste of your endeavours. Since I, Eustace Blount, playwright, satirist, critic, poet, *et cetera*, shall claim the King's prize!"

Suddenly, the other two wits were off their stools and in Eustace's face, poking each other's chests and arguing.

"I shall claim the prize!"

"Nay, I shall claim the prize!"

"Be seated!" came the roar from the rear of the small room. "And be silent!" It was Rose, rising from her armchair.

Like little boys - although they were in their fifties - the three wits ceased their remonstrations, bowed their heads and returned to their stools, shame-faced.

When Abby sidled in beside Jacob, the wits lofted their chins and pinched their noses, as if confronted by a terrible stench.

"Do you smell that, Eustace?" asked one.

"I do, Rupert," he replied. "'Tis as if the River Fleet flowed past my nose!"

A hand slammed down on their table and the proprietor glared.

Upper lip curled into a snarl, Rose told the assembled wits, "One more derogatory word concerning this young woman, who is my guest, and I shall ban the lot of you. Now, make your peace."

Eustace took the proprietor's hand and lightly kissed the back of it. "Mistress," he purred.

When Rupert went to do the same, she snatched it away.

Smirking at his rival, Eustace bade the inquisitors, "Pray, join us," in a tone that suggested he could imagine little worse.

Jacob handed Abby the Exalted Competition of the Arts handbill. "Aye, I know of it," she told him. "Mr Pepys spoke of it. He will be in attendance."

The wits wore matching outfits: black leather shoes with round brass buckles, white stockings, breeches and shirt, except that each wore a different colour coat. Eustace's was crimson, Rupert's was blue, and the third man, Vincent, wore green. All were in varying states of disrepair, and Abby wondered whether there was much money coming in to their respective households.

Rupert and Vincent explained that they were brothers, although they looked nothing like one another. Eustace was almost as tall as Jacob, who was unusually tall; next in height was Rupert; and down to Vincent, who was rather short. So pronounced was the difference in height that their heads could have been used as steps if arranged in the correct order.

Eustace had a sharp, elongated nose and grey eyebrows that were almost as unruly as Jacob's; Rupert's mouth was creased in a permanent sneer; Vincent's face was ruddy, puffy and dripped with sweat, which he was constantly wiping away with a handkerchief.

Once the wits and inquisitors had settled at the table and their dishes were refilled, a simmering, uncomfortable silence descended. Jacob gazed jealously at Abby as she supped her chocolate - which Rose had miraculously managed to concoct, when Abby requested it - licking the thick liquid from her lips.

At length, Eustace spoke up. "I wonder how I shall spend the King's fifty guineas?" he mused aloud.

Rupert snorted. "I have read your work, sir, 'The Resplendent Dawn of our Majestic Kingdom', and I wondered whether it had been penned," he paused for effect, "by a goat."

Eustace took a gulp from a leather flask that was hung around his neck. "And I, sir, have read your work, 'The Regal Splendour and Noble Deeds of His Majesty, King

Charles II, Or This Illuminated Beacon of Hope, Justice, and Benevolence in our Glorious Realm', and consider it to have all the literary merit of... of..."

"Of what, sir?" Rupert asked, inspecting his fingernails.

Cursing under his breath, Eustace rose, picked up his stool and set it on the table. "Of this stool, sir."

"Put that stool back," came Rose's barked order from the back of the room.

Tipping his hat, Eustace meekly obeyed.

Vincent leaned into the table and spoke in a hushed tone. "I fear the trouble," he paused, "is that the King is an ass."

Eustace covered his head with his hands, as if avoiding a swooping bird. Rupert slapped his brother on the cheek, then pointedly wiped his hand.

Vincent remained undeterred. "It is a trial indeed, to glorify the benevolence of a man who is more interested in the contents of his breeches, than he is in the welfare of his subjects."

Eustace grabbed a handful of Vincent's cravat and pulled their faces close together. "With such loose words, the fool loses his head. You seem to forget," he said, nodding sideways towards Abby and Jacob, "that we have guests."

Vincent pushed him away and sat back, sneering. "They are no spies for the King. One is but a girl and the other, I overheard him tell, is the son of Sir Miles Standish, of Standish Hall."

Jacob noticed the wits were staring at him. "Do you suggest that my father was no royalist? Sir Miles Standish was fiercely loyal to the King!"

"Believe what you will," Vincent replied.

Jacob adjusted his periwig. "My father was Surveyor to the King's Navy," he said, causing Rose to look up from her reading. He would have protested further, but the conversation had already returned to the relative merits of the assembled wits' poetry.

Eustace was up on his feet, pointing accusingly at Vincent. "These are his words: 'Oh mighty King, your reign divine. 'Neath you we flourish, like well-aged wine'!" He collapsed into a fit of theatrical giggles. "A child rhymes with greater eloquence, sir!"

His literary opponent rose indignantly, spluttering. "How dare you, sir! Pay heed; *these* are *his* words…"

Chapter Seven

Panic

When Jacob's mind returned to consciousness the following morning, he was elated to realise that he was in his own bed for the first time in weeks. Although his mother, Lady Honoria, may have had many faults (which he would keep to himself), choosing beds and bedding was not among them. Wrapping himself deep inside his embroidered woollen blanket, he went to shift his head and realised his lips had become stuck to his pillow.

It had taken him an age to get to sleep. Pasqua Rosée was not wrong concerning the coffee drink and drowsiness, he thought. "I shall sup no more coffee, as long as I live," he told himself aloud, and resolved to snatch another hour's slumber.

But as he closed his eyes, the church bell of St Clement Danes chimed six. He waited, knowing it was coming... And there it was, the bell of St Mary-le-Strand, reassuringly lagging.

By the time St Mary's sixth ring had echoed into silence, he was wide awake.

Abby, who had heard the church bells chime four, had long been up and about. Although Jacob had offered her the guest chamber, she preferred to sleep in the maid's quarters, on a truckle bed, as she was accustomed to. She had no intention of becoming carried away with herself, in this new-found role as Master Pepys's inquisitor. Too many times in her past, pride had been followed by a fall.

She was plating slices of game pie in the kitchen when Jacob joined her.

"You have food!" he exclaimed, stretching.

"Aye," she replied. "And you did not. How do you survive?"

Snatching a slice, he asked, "Who sold you the pie?"

"The market stalls across The Strand, on Holywell Street. Most were open at dawn; I heard the calls of the traders. I took some coins from your purse while you were snoring and let myself out of the house. I trust you'll not take offence?"

"Not when the pie is this delicious," he replied, chewing thoughtfully, then added, "You say there is a market on Holywell Street?"

"'Tis but 50 yards hence, Jacob! Who purchases your food?"

"The maid."

"The one you dismissed?"

Jacob continued chewing.

The inquisitors settled in the dining room to finish breakfast. Abby had also bought bread, cheese and ale, and both were desperately thirsty.

Rich tapestries and rugs hung on the walls, depicting naval battles and royal galleons under sail. The dining table seated ten on fine-nap upholstered chairs, and the ceiling was plastered, concealing the beams. As Abby and Jacob cut cheese, their knives clinked on their pewter plates, the sound breaking the stiff silence of the space. It made her feel uneasy.

"Are you lonely here?" she asked.

"Nay!" Jacob replied a little too enthusiastically.

"Did your father wish you to marry?"

Jacob shifted in his chair. "What did you make of Vincent's comment, 'Believe what you will'?"

"Concerning your father's political affiliation?"

"Aye, it seemed to me he implied my father's loyalty lay not with the King, which is nonsense. He was loyal to His Majesty till the day he died."

"You should question the wits further."

"Aye," he replied. "I shall. Though 'tis hard to make sense of them."

Abby chuckled and took a slug of her weak ale. "We should return Master Pepys's pocket watch."

"You have it."

"Nay, Jacob, you have it."

He stopped eating and gazed into space. "Aye, I do. It must be in my satchel."

Jacob sprang from his chair and ran upstairs, clearly in a panic.

When he reappeared in the doorway, his long face was white. "I must have left it at the coffee house."

Chapter Eight

The Drained Flask

In the haste to retrace their steps, Jacob and Abby jumped into one of the licensed hackney coaches waiting beneath the maypole outside St Mary-le-Strand Church. Its yellow cab was tapered, wider at the top than at the bottom, and its four wheel-rims were painted red.

While the horses pulling the coach moved at a state pace, it was surely quicker than walking. Abby noticed a difference in the comfort of the journey along Westminster's paved Strand, compared to the rough cobbled streets of the city.

Before the coach had even pulled up outside Rose's, Jacob was out of the door, flicking the driver a shilling coin. "Hurry!" he urged Abby.

As she opened the coffee-house door at street level, she heard him hammering on the one below and calling out anxiously, "Rose! Rose!"

Having made her way carefully down the steep stairs, being sure not to trip over her gown, Abby found the basement door open and stepped inside. The scene that confronted her made her gasp.

Jacob, Rose, Rupert, and Vincent Mortimer were arranged in a circle in the middle of the dimly lit room, staring down at a body.

The body of Eustace Blount.

He was dead, eyes wide open yet glassy, a neat slit in his shirt, fringed with a small red stain.

The position of the body struck Abby as strange; Eustace's arms were stretched out above his head. "Did somebody drag him there?" she asked.

"Aye," Rose replied, her voice dazed.

"Then where was he found?" Abby asked.

Rose and the Mortimer brothers glanced at one another.

"In the privy," said Vincent.

"In the privy?" exclaimed Jacob, adding more solemnly, "That is no place for a gentleman to die."

Rupert crossed himself. "Then we must give thanks that he was no gentleman."

Abby knelt beside the corpse. "When was his body discovered?"

Rose explained that she had opened as usual at six that morning. The wits were already waiting at the door, as was their custom, although, for once, Eustace was not with them.

"Did he usually wait with you?" Abby asked.

"It was he who would arrive first," replied Vincent, taking a seat at his usual table.

"Were you not concerned?" Jacob asked.

Rupert joined his brother. "Not in the slightest."

"I found him when I went to empty the privy," Rose explained.

Abby looked across at the wits. "Did he not leave with you last night?"

Rupert shot Vincent a glance. "The last we saw of him, he was dead drunk. Now," he sniffed haughtily in the direction of Blount's body, "he is merely dead."

The full story gradually emerged.

Unlike the Mortimer brothers, who preferred the calming effects of coffee, Eustace had a predilection for sack. Since Rose refused to sell alcohol, he carried a supply around with him in a flask.

The same leather flask was now lying beside the corpse, still hung around the late wit's neck. Abby picked it up and shook it. It was empty.

Rose told them that just before nine the previous night, when she closed the coffee house, she had found Eustace sound asleep at his table. When he could not be roused, she had no choice but to leave him there to sleep it off, locking both doors behind her. "I have never allowed it before." Glancing at the body, she added bitterly, "And I shall never allow it again."

When she had opened that morning, she continued, not ten minutes before the inquisitors arrived, Eustace was nowhere to be seen. That was when she went out back to check the privy.

The Mortimers had heard her scream, realised something was awry, and here Abby and Jacob found them.

"Who would wish him dead?" asked Jacob.

Everyone besides the inquisitors burst out laughing.

"Sir," Rupert announced, when calm was restored, "as you must surely be aware, Eustace Blount had a mouth the size of the King's libido."

"And he was less popular than the plague," Vincent added, smiling.

Abby searched the body. She found a purse tucked into Eustace's belt, which was empty. "It appears he may have been robbed," she said.

"Jim Quigley?" asked Jacob, bending down beside her. He lifted one of Eustace's hands, then the other. "Black ink?" he suggested, showing her the blackened fingertips of both hands.

Vincent spotted him doing so. "Eustace Blount was a pamphleteer, albeit a mediocre one, as well as a poet, playwright and essayist - talents in which he was equally mediocre," he explained. "That there is ink on his fingers when he spends… I beg your pardon, *spent* his every day handling printed materials, is, I would put to you, unsurprising."

"Yet there is no ink on your fingers, nor on your brother's," Jacob pointed out, "although I noticed there was yesterday. I assume you scrubbed it off."

The Mortimers exchanged wary glances.

Rolling Eustace's body to inspect his back, Jacob continued his examination. "No wound. Thus the weapon must have been short-bladed. I would suggest a dagger," he concluded, pleasantly surprised at how professional he sounded.

Abby stood and addressed Rose, who was staring down at the wit's lifeless form in a state of shock. "Who possesses the keys to the coffee house?"

Rose looked to the Mortimer brothers, who were deep in conversation. "I do," she replied.

"Nobody else?" Abby pressed her.

"Nay, just I." She pointed to her table, on which were two iron keys.

"And both doors were locked when you arrived this morning?"

The proprietor nodded.

Jacob rose and massaged his chin. "Our murderer dispatched Eustace Blount with a dagger and then departed the coffee house, locking both doors behind him."

"Aye, Jacob," said Abby. "Thus he - or she - must have had keys to the property."

Rose realised that everyone was staring at her. "What?" she exclaimed. "Nay! You think that I murdered him?"

No one spoke.

Rose laughed bitterly and went to start the fire in the hearth. "A nincompoop, Eustace Blount may have been, but he was also one of my best customers. That nincompoop's patronage paid my taxes. Why would I murder him? I'm no fool."

Abby pursed her lips.

"We should also ask whether one of these men murdered the poor fellow," Jacob said, waving an accusing finger at the Mortimers. "They freely admit they loathed him."

"How dare you, sir!" exclaimed Rupert, rising from his stool.

"Aye, sir. I should challenge the knave to a duel!" his brother added.

Sensing matters getting out of hand, Abby gestured for calm. "Hold your tongue!" she scolded her fellow inquisitor. "Only a fool speculates, Jacob."

An uneasy silence lingered.

Suddenly, the basement door, left unlocked amid the commotion, flew open, and a tiny old man burst in. He wore a brightly coloured, diamond-patterned Harlequin doublet and carried an unwieldy leather case. Though bald, a tail of wispy white hair trailed down his back, and his wizened face belied a sprightly demeanour.

"I came as quickly as I could!" he said in a brittle voice. When he spotted the body of Eustace Blount lying on the floor, he exclaimed, "Oh my!" and put a hand to his mouth.

Rose looked up from her fireside duties. "Zebulon Strangeway," she said. "What brings you here?"

The inquisitors both noticed the dagger sheathed in his belt.

Chapter Nine

Zebulon Strangeway

"A messenger boy found me," Strangeway explained, seated at the wits' table with Abby and Jacob. "He told me I must visit Rose's Coffee House with all haste."

"Who sent him?" asked Abby.

"He would not say," the old man replied. "However I have my suspicions."

"What are your suspicions?" Jacob asked.

Strangeway peered at him through silvery eyes, beneath which were extravagant, dark bags. "I beg your pardon, sir, but who are you?"

Jacob rolled out his patter. "We are the personal inquisitors of Mr Samuel Pepys, who is Clerk of the Acts to the Navy Board," he replied. "And you, sir, are the peddler of quack medicines whose handbills are to be found upon these walls."

"You do me a grave injustice, sir," said Strangeway, rising to perform a pirouette. Pushing out a foot, Rupert

Mortimer tripped the old man, sending him tumbling to the floor.

"Leave him be!" Rose called out angrily from her armchair.

When Abby moved to help the quack up, he brushed her aside, muttering curses at the wit, who was struggling to contain his glee.

Retaking his seat, he opened his case and handed Jacob a sheet of paper. The inquisitor noticed that his fingernails were ingrained with dirt.

Zebulon Strangeway's
Liberty Elixir

A most excellent remedy for mental fog and subservience. An ointment for the head concocted from black hellebore and several other esteemed ingredients noted for their intellectual properties.
Stimulates clarity of thought and free will.
Price one shilling.

Jacob spluttered mockingly. "Liberty Elixir! A remedy for mental fog and subservience! What nonsense is this?"

"Confound it!" Strangeway exclaimed, snatching the paper back. "'Twas the wrong handbill."

"Mr Strangeway possesses a cure for all known ailments, do you not, Zebulon?" said Vincent. "Scrofula, the

King's Evil, consumption, convulsions, smallpox, griping in the guts…"

"Ah!" his brother cut in, pointing at Eustace's corpse. "But can he cure death?"

"I am indeed working on such a cure," Strangeway assured him, "though I shall not divulge my secrets."

Rupert nudged his brother. "Does it require woodlice boiled in oil? Since all your remedies do!" The wits dissolved into giggles.

As the rich, bittersweet aroma of coffee reached everyone's noses, they noticed that Rose was roasting beans over her fire. Although she appeared intent on her task, Abby felt certain that she was taking in their conversation.

"Hurry, woman!" Rupert called to her. "Proximity to death, I have discovered, only exacerbates my thirst."

"I must say," said Strangeway, reaching out to kick the sole of Eustace's shoe, causing the cadaver to judder, "he is far more agreeable in death than he ever was in life."

"Aye, sir," said Rupert, applauding. "I would drink to that… If I had one."

"You didn't like him?" Abby asked the quack.

"He lampooned my profession."

"And what, pray, do you consider to be your profession?" Jacob asked.

"Why, sir, I am a physician," Strangeway replied, to the great mirth of the surviving wits. "I have in my possession a medical licence, granted to me by the Royal College of Physicians." Glancing perfunctorily inside his bag, he concluded, "However I appear to have left it at home."

Rupert sucked on his clay pipe and blew smoke into Strangeway's face. "And yet he wears the garb of a fool."

"As well you know, my distinctive garb brings me to people's attention," the quack replied. "It is my stock in trade, sir."

"Aye, the trade of a wily old fox," said Vincent.

Rose poured out steaming black coffee from an engraved brass pot with a thin, curved spout. As she reached Abby's bowl, she stopped. "Fear not, my dear," she said. "I shall make chocolate for you."

Abby smiled at her, and she returned the gesture.

Jacob regarded his drink with disdain. "I cannot help but notice your dagger, Mr Strangeway," he said, fishing a floating coffee ground from his bowl. "May I see it?"

"You believe I killed Eustace Blount? That this weapon caused that wound?" Strangeway asked, nodding towards the corpse. Unsheathing the knife, he held it out before him, turning the blade for all to see. "You must understand, I use this knife only for good. It cuts herbs and plants for my pills and salves, and makes incisions in the sick for blood-letting, that I may balance their humours of blood, choler, yellow and black bile."

"Does that explain the blood I spy there upon its blade?" asked Jacob.

"I used it this morning to slice fresh mutton!" Strange-way snapped, hastily returning the weapon to its sheath.

Abby touched Jacob's sleeve. "We should investigate the privy," she told him quietly.

Chapter Ten

The Ghost of St Robert

*I*n the Kelburne house, the shutters were closed on any talk of Guy Fawkes. It only made Anne's son more determined to discover who his uncle was, and why the mere mention of his name caused a room to fall silent.

George Lund was happy to oblige. He told Guy of the Gunpowder Treason Plot to assassinate King James I. The plan involved igniting dozens of barrels of gunpowder secreted in the undercroft beneath the House of Lords during the State Opening of Parliament on November 5*th* 1605. Many men – Commons and Lords alike – would have died, not just the King. It was a sacrifice the conspirators were prepared to make in their fanatical bid to rid England of its anti-Catholic king.

Among their number was a Yorkshireman named Guy Fawkes, George explained, who was charged with igniting the gunpowder. He was Anne Kelburne's brother and Guy's uncle.

"What became of him?" Guy asked.

George shook his head bitterly. "Have you heard the church bells ring every November the fifth?" When Guy said he had *not, he continued, "'Tis to celebrate the thwarting of the plot. Your uncle was captured – betrayed, 'tis believed, by one of his own – and executed."*

Guy shuddered.

George placed a calloused hand on his shoulder and looked the boy in the eye. "He was a good man, your uncle. I will never celebrate his demise. But you must be wary, Guy. The King's spies are everywhere and seek any reason to persecute we Catholics. King Charles is no better than King James, mark my words. 'Tis why your father and mother will not speak of Guy Fawkes, for they are afraid."

Guy began to misbehave.

He told his mother he wanted to be a recusant Catholic like George Lund, and refused to attend the local Anglican church service. She tried reasoning with him, pointing out that the £20 fine was a devastating amount, and that they did not wish to attract the attention of the local church warden, nor the Justice of the Peace, not with their family name.

"If the name Guy Kelburne becomes entered upon the Recusant Rolls," she told him, "it would be the ruin of this family."

When he chose not to hear sense, she boxed his ears and his father dragged him to church.

Only to himself would Guy admit that his stand had less to do with any religious fervour – frankly, he found the sermons boring – than with a desire to challenge authority.

By the time he was a teenager, Guy could have run his father's mill by himself, so familiar was he with the flour-making process and with every nook and cranny.

He had helped to winnow and sieve the grain, cleaning it prior to milling; he had helped resurface the two huge millstones with a chisel to maximise the grinding power. As he grew strong enough, he would heave each grain sack onto his shoulder and tip the contents into the mill's hopper, which fed the grain into the millstones.

He knew the purpose of every wheel, shaft and gear. He could have repaired any breakdown or fashioned any spare part from wood.

But the old man was cautious and liked doing things his way.

One morning, when the sails of the windmill seemed to be turning unusually laconically, despite a reasonable breeze, Henry went outside to find Guy clinging to the tip of the topmost sail, some seventy feet off the ground.

"I'm helping to turn the sails!" Guy called down, waggling his feet provocatively.

When the sails returned the boy to his raging father, he was locked in the grain store overnight, with no dinner or supper.

News of the foolhardy act spread around his home village of Scotton, causing Guy to become feted among his peer group. He began to accept challenges to accomplish further feats of daring.

Although he could not swim, Guy would accept halfpenny wagers to leap from the high Grimbald Bridge into the deep, dark water of the River Nidd. On one occasion, his foot became entangled in reeds, and he was lucky to be rescued by a passing boatman.

One night when he was eighteen, as a result of another such challenge, Guy slept overnight in St Robert's Cave. There were rumours that the place was haunted by the ghost of St Robert himself, a hermit who had lived there some centuries ago.

The cave, carved into a limestone cliff on the bank of the River Nidd, was in the neighbouring town of Knaresborough, less than two miles away. To bolster his courage, Guy stole a flagon of ale from his mother, and to add spice to the adventure, he donned a dark old hooded robe of his father's, such as he imagined St Robert might have worn.

If the ghost would not appear to him, Guy reasoned, he would play the ghost.

A few friends accompanied him as he descended the well-worn stone steps down towards the cave. The river flowed past to their left, and overhanging boughs from the surrounding woodland brushed their faces. The steep riverbank was covered in ivy.

The cave itself was barely the size of a shepherd's hut, and cold. Guy was glad of the robe as he began concocting tales of the hermit's hauntings for his friends' entertainment.

As the sun set, the light of a full moon began to cast sinister shadows. The night creatures emerged. There were rustlings in the undergrowth and unfamiliar animal calls from up in the trees.

One by one, Guy's friends made their excuses and left, until he was all alone in the cave. Shivering, he realised he had forgotten to bring a lantern and downed the last of the ale.

Feeling quite light-headed, he lay down on the hard stone floor and began drifting off to sleep. That was when he heard the footsteps through the undergrowth, accompanied by low whispers and giggling. Peeking out of the cave, he saw two dark figures – a man and a woman, from their voices – heading towards him.

If they're coming to the cave at this late hour, *he thought to himself,* I can imagine their intentions.

As the couple reached the cave entrance, Guy pulled the hood down over his face and walked out, moaning deeply, arms aloft.

They may well have heard the screams back in Scotton.

Chuckling to himself, with a new tale to tell that could only heighten his growing reputation, Guy returned to the cave and dozed off.

The next morning, sleeping off a hangover, he found himself violently prodded awake.

The Knaresborough constable took a dim view of Guy's antics. He had scared the wits out of the local landowner's son (who had apparently omitted to mention his companion). As a punishment, Guy was put in the stocks in the market square, with a sign around his neck that read:

I am the false ghost of St Robert

He was still wearing the robe.

Most passers-by laughed, some cat-called, and a few tossed rotten fruit and vegetables. Guy's cheeky expression, since he refused to be cowed, meant that nobody threw stones or anything more dangerous – a fate that had befallen many a previous occupant.

Only one person spoke to him. A young woman around his age, she appeared to him as a vision of beauty, with black hair tied up beneath a cotton coif and eyes that glowed like sunlight trapped in amber.

She spoke into his ear to ensure she was not overheard. "I know your name," she told him. "My father was involved with your uncle in the Gunpowder Treason Plot."

Chapter Eleven

The Privy

J acob was about to open the rear side door of the coffee house, which led to the privy, when he glanced at Rose's effects on the shelves behind her. Among the piles of old pamphlets on her bookshelf, he saw several expensive, leather-bound books with gilt edging.

The proprietor, who was cracking egg-yolk into a wooden bowl filled with milk and water, eyed him with suspicion. "That is my private library, Mr Standish," she told him. "I will thank you for keeping your hands off it."

The book titles meant little to him, but Abby had seen them too and recognised several from Mr Pepys's own shelves. Among the most notable were *Eikon Basilike*, written by King Charles I himself, and *Leviathan*, by Thomas Hobbes. Both volumes, she knew, advocated rule by an absolute sovereign and were deemed fervently monarchist. *Yet*, she thought, *Rose's clientele appears to be republicans. Why, Vincent Mortimer even spoken ill of the King.*

Bluntly, she asked the proprietor, "Are you for King or Parliament?"

Rose narrowed her eyes, smirking. "You're an astute little one, Abigail Harcourt."

"Which is it?" Abby persisted.

The proprietor crumbled a block of cocoa into her bowl, adding star anise, vanilla, cinnamon and a pinch of cayenne pepper. "I bear no preference," she said. "Let men fight their wars. I need only their patronage and their money." She paused, stirring. "Any more impertinent questions and I'll sell your chocolate to the wits."

Once through the side door, the inquisitors found themselves in a short, wood-panelled corridor lit by two flickering candles, one on either side of the privy door facing them. So ill-lit was it that their pale, illuminated faces appeared to float, disembodied, in the darkness.

Jacob took one of the candles and explored the space. To his right, the corridor ended abruptly; to his left, it continued for some five yards.

Jacob lifted the privy latch and stepped inside. There was the bench with a hole cut into it, suspended over a wooden bucket. The pervading odour was necessarily potent.

"Did you believe her?" Abby called in.

"Concerning what?"

"Concerning her loyalties."

So absorbed was he in his inspection of the compacted-clay floor, that he failed to reply.

"Nought," he said when he rejoined his fellow inquisitor. "What did we expect to find?"

Abby laid out the facts. No one liked Eustace Blount, she said, which made everyone a potential suspect. The greatest puzzle was that he appeared to have been murdered in a locked room.

"What of suicide?" Jacob asked.

"Then we would have found a weapon," she pointed out. "Yet you found nought in the privy. If Eustace was indeed murdered, the murderer must have had the keys both to the street-level door and the basement."

"Yet Rose claims to possess the only ones."

"Aye, Jacob. 'Tis a quandary."

"Unless 'twas her who committed the murderous deed?"

"Or she's lying about the keys, and somebody else has a set?"

Idly, Jacob began peering at the walls, holding his candle close to see better. "Why does the corridor continue in this direction?" he muttered to himself. "Yet it ends in a wall?"

"It may have been dug out many years ago, and the panelling later added," Abby suggested. "Who knows what was once here."

"Precisely," he replied, tapping at the panels along the two longest walls. The sounds that returned were dull thuds.

Suddenly, his attention was drawn elsewhere. Bending down, he placed his candle on the floor. "What are these?" he asked, tracing his fingertips along two thin, parallel track-marks in the clay floor. Following them, he saw that they ended abruptly at the far wall.

The inquisitors looked at each other quizzically.

Jacob tapped the wood panelling above the disappearing tracks. "Hollow!" he exclaimed.

When he pushed the lowest panel, a hidden door swung open, swivelling on a horizontal axis. The top half of the door swung down into their section of the corridor, while the lower half disappeared into a newly revealed extension.

From his crouch, Jacob stared up at Abby.

"There's more to Rose's Coffee House than meets the eye," she said, grinning.

They crawled beneath the door. The track marks continued into a corridor that stretched into darkness. The air was dank and stale, and the silence was broken by the slow, echoing drip of water.

Jacob spotted an oil lamp affixed to a wall and lit it using his candle flame. Its warm glow revealed the space around them.

The new corridor was panelled identically to the section in Rose's, suggesting it had once been a single length, later divided by the secret door. Some 15 or 20 yards ahead, a closed curtain marked the far end; beside it, an alcove receded into the shadows.

In the wall to their right, a section of panelling had been removed at floor level, revealing a compact alcove - a yard square and deep - carved from the clay. Opposite that was a door, the track-marks on the floor leading beneath it.

"Shall we try the door?" Abby asked.

Jacob nodded.

The sight that greeted the inquisitors astonished them.

"What can it be?" asked Jacob.

Abby was already examining the machine. She had seen one before, as a child. Her father had operated it, and she had helped him. "'Tis a printing press," she told him, caressing its smooth wooden surface. "It must have been built here, piece by piece. Quite an achievement."

The imposing structure stood ten feet tall, its upright frame made of thick wooden beams, supporting a horizontal bed where printing plates were laid. As the large screw within the frame was turned, Abby explained, a rectangular wooden block pressed down onto the inked printing plate, transferring the design onto paper.

The inquisitors could smell the ink. The press had been used – recently.

The room's walls were clay. Heavy wooden beams supported the ceiling, which was significantly higher than that of the corridor, to accommodate the tall printing press. In the centre of the ceiling was a wooden grille, about two feet square. "An old air grate," Jacob suggested.

Elsewhere were screwed-up balls of paper, piled pamphlets and handbills, and a table covered in ink jars, brushes and tools. Around the walls, as in the coffee house itself, were plastered printed materials of varying sizes and age.

Abby took the oil lamp, held it close to one wall and read aloud the titles of the attached handbills. "'The Hidden Truth - Revealing Corruption in the Court of King Charles'; 'A Most Earnest Appeal to Parliament for the Restoration of True Liberty'; 'A Manifesto for the Downtrodden'... Jacob," she said, "this is treason. The men responsible would hang."

"The wits," he said.

"Aye. It seems I underestimated them."

"I did not. As seditious a group of rogues as any gentleman might wish to meet. I will delight in seeing them hang."

Abby's determined expression was framed in the lantern's golden glow. "I suggest you keep your views to yourself, Jacob. 'Tis wise to keep one's counsel among strangers." As she spoke, something on the wall caught her eye. "See here - names scratched in the clay." Peering closely, she read them out. "John Fryer and Harry... nay, Henry Corbet."

"We know of no such men," said Jacob. "Perhaps their names were etched there long ago."

"They seem more recent than that."

There was a handbill lying on the print-bed, and Jacob picked it up. "Since Eustace's fingers were blackened with ink, we may assume this was the handbill he was printing on the day his death."

Scanning it first, he handed it to Abby. It read:

Citizens, Arise!
Resist the King's Public Order & Safety Bill!

This Bill is an attack upon our freedoms. It seeks to control our gatherings, censor our speech, and monitor our lives under the pretence of public safety.

The Bill's True Intentions:
Close our meeting places.
Censor our printed materials.
Assault our free expression.
Intimidate and suppress.

Shame on Culpepper! Shame on Davenport! Shame on the King!

Resist the Bill!
Defend our right to assemble and to speak freely.

"Is that the reason he was murdered?" Jacob asked.

"Aren't Culpepper and Davenport the same men who sponsored the King's Arts Challenge?"

"I believe they are."

Abby tucked the handbill into her satchel. "Let's have a look around," she said.

"Will the wits not grow suspicious?" he asked. "We have lingered here a while."

"Such is their self-regard, I doubt they've even noticed we are gone. Rose is another matter. You're right, Jacob, we should indeed make haste."

"Hold," he said, raising his arm. "Hand me the lamp."

Kneeling, he studied the floor and saw that the track marks they had followed into the printing room ended abruptly in the middle of the room. "Those must be Eustace's heel marks," he said, "made when he was dragged from this spot."

"So he was murdered here?"

Jacob pointed out a few dark spots in the clay, clustered inside a circular indentation, about two feet in diameter. "I would wager that is the poor fellow's blood."

"You're becoming an excellent inquisitor, Jacob," Abby told him. "Now, we must hurry back to the coffee house, ere we're discovered."

He stopped her. "Nay. We should continue. There are other secrets to be discovered."

As she glanced nervously toward the door, he took her hand. "Trust me," he said.

Jacob thrust the oil lamp into the small alcove opposite the door to the printing room. "Coins," he said, "scattered here among dirt."

"Pocket them quickly, Jacob," she hissed. "I'm sure I heard a door open."

He strode quickly to the far end of the corridor, Abby close behind, and whisked aside the curtain. "'Tis but a storage space," he muttered. Inside was the usual clutter: a broom, a large barrel, planks of wood, a ladder, shovel, coiled rope, a rusty old hammer and chisel…

Turning to his right, he found himself facing the alcove they had seen from the other end of the corridor. Now, he could see it contained a steep set of steps leading up to a trap-door. A battered old brush and an empty sack lay at the foot of the steps.

"Zounds!" Jacob exclaimed.

"That trap-door will not open," came a woman's voice.

"How would you…?" he began, then realised the voice was not Abby's.

"I've tried it myself and it will not budge," Rose added. She was standing beside the printing room door, her features radiating in candlelight.

As she made her way towards the inquisitors, Jacob blurted out, "We are the personal inquisitors of Mr Samuel Pepys…"

She cut him off. "I know who you are. And by the by, I've never heard of your Samuel Pepys."

Jacob glanced back up at the trap-door.

Rose stopped and held her candle up to his face. "If you don't believe me, try it."

He needed no further invitation.

Ascending the steps, with outstretched hands he pushed at the trap-door, grunting with exertion. The iron-hinged door refused to budge.

He tried again and again, but eventually had to admit defeat. "It will not give even an inch," he said, descending the steps.

Rose smiled at him. "Why would you not believe me, Mr Standish?"

"It pays to be suspicious," Abby replied.

"Where does the door lead?" Jacob asked.

"Since I have never opened it, I wouldn't know." Before he could interject, Rose continued, "I estimate that it leads to The Gilded Bean coffee house, situated behind mine, on St Martin's Lane."

"You knew of this secret corridor," Abby stated.

"Naturally," she purred, taking a lock of Abby's red hair and twisting it around her finger. "I opened this coffee shop in 1658. It was inevitable I would find it."

Jacob grabbed her arm. "And you permit its use for seditious purposes," he snapped.

Rose released Abby's hair, her face hardening as she glared at him. "You would do well to forget what you saw here, inquisitor - lest the forces that hastened Eustace Blount's demise turn themselves upon you."

He pushed his face in hers. "You know the identity of these forces?"

Rose threw her head back and cackled. "Don't be a fool! Why would I?"

"Who are John Fryer and Henry Corbet?" Abby asked.

If the question unsettled the proprietor, it was only for a fleeting moment. "Patrons of my establishment, who spend their pennies no more," she said. "Since they were executed for treason. You see, Mr Standish, danger stalks this place. Speak of what you found here to no one, on pain of death." Then she took Abby's hand. "Come, my dear. Your chocolate grows cold."

Chapter Twelve

The Rug

When Abby and Jacob re-entered Rose's through the rear door, both gazed fearfully towards Rupert and Vincent Mortimer. They need not have worried. The wits were so raucously engaged in pompous debate that they would not have noticed the inquisitors had they emerged juggling.

Rose, too, ignored them, as they walked past her and stepped over Eustace's untended body.

Selecting the table furthest from the Mortimers, both sat heavily. They were wide-eyed and exhausted.

Neither spoke while Rose placed a bowl of chocolate and another of coffee before them.

Jacob shook his head and laced his fingers together, elbows on the table. "Fie," he said quietly.

"Aye," Abby replied, exhaling. "This is an investigation like no other."

Jacob glanced surreptitiously across at the wits, then back at her. "What shall we do?"

She took his hand and squeezed it. "We do nought."

He was about to reply when she put her finger to her lips. "Rose speaks the truth," she hissed. "Men will die if we breathe a word of what we have seen."

"They deserve to die," he hissed back, "for treason."

"Nay, Jacob. Ours is not to judge, but to investigate and determine guilt. We must allow others to judge."

"But they are guilty!" he insisted, too loudly, and they both once again glanced at the self-absorbed wits.

Abby released Jacob's hand. "We should leave."

There came two knocks on the door. The wits fell silent.

All eyes followed Rose as she walked to the door, unlocked and opened it.

In stepped Jim Quigley, followed by another, bedraggled man who looked as though he slept in alleyways. Between them, they were carrying a long, heavy rolled-up rug.

Quigley nodded at Rose. "Good morrow!" he said cheerily. "I hear there is an unfortunate…" Spotting Eustace, he dropped his burden and crossed himself. "Ah, indeed, poor Mr Blount. He will be sorely missed."

"Like gout," Rupert piped up.

Briefly acknowledging Abby and Jacob, Quigley retrieved the rug, and he and his companion set it down beside the body. Watched in stunned silence - the wits feigned indifference - he removed Eustace's leather shoes and handed them to his companion, who shoved them into a sack. Then he started on the dead man's rings.

"Those are mine," snapped Vincent. "I bought them for him, and he owes me money, so I shall have them." When Quigley stared at him sceptically, he added, "Or should we discuss the matter with the alderman?"

Reluctantly, the old thief handed over the jewellery.

"You may keep whatever of his attire you so wish," Vincent added sniffily. "I always said that he dressed like a fop." That he was dressed identically had escaped his notice.

Casting an expert eye over the body, Quigley reached for the dead man's hat and periwig. Placing them upon his head, he proceeded to admire himself in an imaginary looking-glass. Next, he removed the lace-trimmed cravat, which was worth a few shillings.

Jacob yelped. "His neck is bruised!" he exclaimed, pointing.

Indeed, a thick earthy-brown band encircling Eustace's neck was now clear for all to see.

Abby rubbed her freckled cheeks vigorously. *Was he strangled also?* she wondered.

Outside, Quigley and his companion heaved Eustace's body, concealed in the rolled rug, into the back of a horse-drawn cart, watched by the inquisitors.

"Are you an undertaker now?" Jacob asked witheringly.

Quigley tipped his new hat. "Nay, Mr Standish. I deliver rugs."

"Rugs with dead men inside?"

Quigley patted the rug. "No dead men here, sir."

And off he went, handing his companion, who was heading in the opposite direction, a halfpenny for his trouble.

"Utter scoundrel," Jacob muttered to himself, as he and Abby stood on The Strand at the bottom of St Martin's Lane. "We ought to have had him arrested."

"Forget Quigley," said Abby. "I believe Eustace was strangled to death, not stabbed."

"Why?"

"In his library, Master Pepys keeps the work *De Motu Cordis* by the physician William Harvey. The title translates to *On…*"

"*The Motion of the Heart and Blood.* Aye, I studied Latin."

"Its content meant little to us, however I recall that Harvey wrote of the heart pumping blood through the body."

Jacob shrugged, bewildered.

"There was but a small amount of blood at the wound, Jacob," she went on. "Eustace's heart had already stopped when it was made. *He was strangled to death.*"

"Then why use the dagger?"

Abby shook her head. "I have no idea."

"Neither I."

She motioned up St Martin's Lane. "Shall we pay a visit to The Gilded Bean?"

Jacob noticed that Westminster had come to life during their time at Rose's. *A better sort of citizen walks the streets here*, he mused. *Men of great virtue and renown, their delicate ladies lavishly attired in silk bodices and low-cut gowns. The city where Abby resides is overrun with hackney coaches and throngs of people, yet here one is as likely to see a single gentleman carried in a sedan chair by chairmen in the finest livery…*

"I said, 'Shall we pay a visit to the Gilded Bean?'" Abby repeated.

"Forgive me," he replied. "Aye."

Having followed the outer wall of Rose's Coffee House, they arrived at an unassuming manor house. In the courtyard, two men were tending a horse. There was no signage for a coffee house but, through the leaded windows of the next building, they could see men in hats and periwigs gathered inside.

"The Gilded Bean?" Jacob asked.

"There," one of the men replied, pointing to the building where the men were gathered. "'Twas once part of this house."

The church bell of St Martin's-in-the-Fields, further up the lane, chimed eight. Across the road, one of the horses at the King's stables in Royal Mews began whinnying, disturbed by the clanging.

"What do we seek once we are inside?" Jacob asked Abby.

"The trap-door," she replied. "It must be in there somewhere." Abby explained her reasoning: if the trap-door could only be opened from above, having perhaps been bolted shut inside The Gilded Bean, then the murderer must have come from there. "That is, if Rose indeed has the only set of keys."

Chapter Thirteen

The Gilded Bean

The door to The Gilded Bean was heavy oak, painted black, with iron stud-work. Its sign, nailed above the door, depicted a golden coffee bean above a plain white porcelain bowl. The paintwork looked fresh and the woodwork solid, in stark contrast to the entrance to Rose's. Clearly, this was an establishment of a higher standing altogether.

Jacob entered first. The gentlemen seated inside - and they were all gentlemen, given their expensive clothing - around half a dozen large round tables paid him little heed, merely the odd cursory glance. They were too wrapped up in their braying conversations, some standing and pontificating, others belly-laughing with false joviality, the majority smoking pipes. A boy, smartly attired, was weaving between the tables, filling empty coffee bowls.

When Abby followed Jacob inside, the place fell death-ly silent. She could feel her cheeks reddening, and lowered her head to avoid anyone's gaze. It was the situation she had dreaded.

One tall gentleman rose from his chair, pointing the end of his silver-topped cane at her. He wore a deep-red velvet coat with gold edging, a wide-brimmed hat bearing three white feathers, and his flouncy lace cravat matched his protruding sleeves. "Away with you, woman!" he called out in a strange, nasal voice.

The man next to him then stood as well. He was much shorter and stockier, wearing a similarly ostentatious periwig, although his hat bore five feathers, all in different colours. He wore a sword at his side, which he looked incapable of wielding. "No women here!" he bellowed and looked around, wafting his hands, encouraging others to join in.

"No women here! No women here!" The chant grew as his fellow patrons partook, stomping their polished leather boots on the floor and slapping the tables with their elegantly gloved hands. "No women here! No women here!"

Abby looked up at Jacob, and he saw that her eyes were welling up. "Stay," she hissed, then fled up the stairs.

"Bravo, sir!" came the cries as the Gilded Bean patrons applauded the two gentlemen who had confronted such a wanton outrage.

Jacob suddenly felt very alone. He had become so used to Abby's company – and intellectual support – that he felt lost without it.

He glanced around the room. Everyone had returned to their conversations, as if he no longer existed. The Gilded Bean was twice the size of Rose's, with a grander fireplace and ornately carved furniture. Its walls were plastered not only with printed matter but with rich men's trappings: muskets, swords, coats of arms, stuffed beasts. Knights and kings, in gilt-framed portraits, appeared to glare down at him.

The largest portrait was of King Charles II, and beside that, one of his father, Charles I. Jacob could see no portrait of Oliver Cromwell. The men gathered here were ardent royalists, he surmised, far removed politically from the republicans of Rose's. Jacob shared his father's loyalties and knew which he preferred: the supporters of his beloved King.

At the far end of the room was a deep counter, covered in coffee-making equipment and accessories: a mortar and pestle, bowls and spoons, and sacks of dark-brown beans that had been roasted over the fire. There was a man standing in front of it, conversing intently with another behind it (no doubt, the proprietor). The former was wearing a brightly coloured, diamond-pattern Harlequin outfit and carrying an unwieldy leather case. *Zebulon*

Strangeway! Jacob realised, delighted to encounter a familiar face, even if it had to be Strangeway's.

Emboldened, he strode to the counter. Abby had told him to find the trap-door, so that is what he would do.

The proprietor was perusing a handbill with Strangeway when Jacob sidled up, towering over the pair of them. Upon noticing the inquisitor, he snatched the paper away and pushed it under his counter. However, Jacob had already recognised it.

"The King's Arts Challenge," he said breezily. "Do you intend to enter?"

"What business is that of yours?" came the proprietor's curt reply.

"Mr Standish!" Strangeway exclaimed. "The personal inquisitor of… What was the gentleman's name, pray?"

"Mr Samuel Pepys, who is Clerk of the Acts to the Navy Board."

"A powerful man indeed," the quack pointed out.

The old proprietor looked Jacob up and down through tired blue eyes, distaste curled upon his lips. There was a door and a wall-mounted set of cubby-holes behind him, like that at Rose's, although here several of the compartments contained documents. "I'm Thomas Thackery, owner of The Gilded Bean," he said, with a Londoner's burr. "What's your business 'ere?"

"Why, sir, the business of coffee!" Jacob replied, not wishing to give his game away.

Thackery was a slovenly-looking man, yet muscular and wiry - not to be trifled with. His appearance - billowing cotton shirt, hanging out over breeches with holes in the knees - belied that of his establishment. He was bald on top with wispy, grey-streaked dark hair at the back and sides; his chin was unshaven and his rough hands were stained dark-brown, Jacob assumed from the grinding of his roasted beans.

Strangeway reached into his bag and passed the inquisitor a handbill. "I was about to offer Mr Thackery some of my advertisements for display," he said. "Would you care to read? It is my most popular concoction."

Zebulon Strangeway's Miracle Tonic
Restore Your Vitality!

A wondrous elixir to cure all ailments.
Relieves aches and pains.
Restores energy and vigour.
Purifies the blood.
Made from the finest secret ingredients.
Only 2 shillings per bottle.

Once Jacob had read it, the quack added, "If I may be so bold, you do appear somewhat dour and in need of some vitality." He handed Jacob a small, green-glass corked bottle labelled 'Zebulon Strangeway's Miracle Tonic'. "It will also prolong your lifespan. I myself swear by it."

Jacob held it up to the light. *Are those woodlice?* he wondered. "You yourself take this tonic?" he asked incredulously.

"Indeed, sir, and look at me." Strangeway pirouetted. "I am ninety-nine years of age, would you believe?"

"Nay, I would not," Jacob replied, returning the bottle to the old man.

Suddenly, the room fell silent.

Has Abby dared to return? Jacob wondered.

In the doorway was Rose, holding Abby by the shoulders in front of her. The inquisitor looked uneasy.

The Gilded Bean's patrons began jeering, and Rose shouted over them. "If this young woman is good enough for my coffee house, Thomas Thackery, then she is good enough for yours!"

A cacophony of cat-calls and guffaws broke out.

"I do as my patrons wish!" Thackery bellowed back. "And they don't wish to see her!"

A great cheer rose up, accompanied by much table-slapping and foot-stomping.

Leaving Abby behind, Rose marched up to the table occupied by the two men who had caused the inquisitor's sorry exit in the first place. "What say you, Culpepper?"

Jacob caught Abby's eye; both had noticed the man's name. It was associated with the King's Arts Challenge and with His Majesty's Public Order & Safety Bill.

"How dare you, idle wench! 'Tis *Mr* Culpepper to you!" Culpepper snapped.

"Then what say you," Rose curtseyed mockingly, "*Mr* Culpepper?"

The jeering recommenced, including a number of lewd comments that suggested Culpepper may have had designs upon the coffee-house proprietor.

When the racket subsided, Culpepper stared at Rose, his hollow cheeks reddening. "You would do well to remember your place!" he thundered, to several theatrical intakes of breath. "Or would you prefer to jeopardise your liberty?"

Rose pursed her lips provocatively. "Did I not introduce my companion?" With her hand at her side, she surreptitiously beckoned Abby to join her.

The inquisitor did so as if enduring a walk of shame, glancing uneasily about her at the sweaty, leering faces, her fists clenching and unclenching. Rose took her once again by the shoulders and held her out in front of Culpepper.

"This young woman," Rose announced, "is the personal inquisitor of Mr Samuel Pepys."

"He is Clerk of the Acts to the Navy Board," Jacob piped up helpfully from the back of the room.

"We know who Pepys is!" came a gruff reply.

Culpepper rose angrily, his knuckles whitening on the table. "Such nonsense you do speak!" he snapped. "Mr Pepys would never employ…" He looked Abby up and down with palpable disdain. "*That!*"

"'Tis true, sir!" Jacob called out. "I, too, am Mr Pepys's personal inquisitor. He thinks most highly of Mistress Harcourt. He…"

All heads swivelled to view Jacob, and he clammed up.

"Is what that man says true?" Culpepper demanded, glaring at Abby.

"Aye, sir." It came out so timidly, she cleared her throat and repeated herself. "Aye, sir. 'Tis the truth."

Culpepper sneered and glanced down at his seated companion, who could only shrug. "Then I suggest we put it to a vote!" he announced. "All those in favour of allowing this woman to remain in The Gilded Bean, raise your hand!"

A smattering of hands went up. As others saw their friends and colleagues doing so, several more - if hesitantly - followed suit. However, some did not. Culpepper cast his gimlet eyes around the room, his lips moving quickly as he totted up the votes under his breath.

Abby glanced around; it would be a tight call. Her temples throbbed.

When the votes were counted, Culpepper called for silence. "Esteemed Members of Parliament!" he bellowed.

"The result of the vote is thus… Ayes: twelve. Nays: eleven. I fear," he let his head drop, "she remains."

Eleven men booed, twelve cheered.

Chapter Fourteen

Out Back

With relief, Abby joined Jacob at the counter. She clutched his coat sleeve while she regained her composure. *Why have I let these awful men upset me?* she wondered. *Was it not I who told Jacob to heed lightly the words of men who crave power?*

Zebulon Strangeway tapped her on the shoulder. "Fear not," he said gently, "They loathe me also."

"They are Members of Parliament?" Jacob asked.

"Aye," Strangeway replied. "And a few lawyers. Each bears a common characteristic."

Jacob was eventually obliged to ask, "What is this characteristic?"

"They are foppish louts, Mr Standish. Yet cunning."

One gentleman at the nearest table must have overheard Strangeway's words, since he turned and addressed the coffee-house proprietor angrily. "Mr Thackery, when will you ban this quack? His presence offends me, sir."

"Aye," another at the same table agreed. "And he distributes seditious literature!"

"Nay, sir," countered Strangeway, scurrying to his accuser and opening his bag for him to see inside. "All I possess are advertisements for my ointments and elixirs, which have cured great men such as yourself of the most grievous ailments." Selecting a glass vial from his bag, he held it up. "See here, Zebulon Strangeway's Wondrous Remedy for…"

His accuser swiped it away, and it shattered against a wall.

"Oh, sir, nay!" groaned the quack, dropping to his knees. "That restorative was valued at two shillings."

"If you do not ban this seditious charlatan, Mr Thackery, I shall take my custom elsewhere," the accuser declared.

Thackery glanced at Strangeway. "Sir Montague, I'd remind you that London's other coffee houses of repute were destroyed in the fire. Or perhaps you'd rather take your custom to Rose's?"

"Bah!" Sir Montague exclaimed with a dismissive wave of his hand, and returned to his conversation.

Abby noticed a small square table in a dark corner, on which Thackery told them he counted the day's takings. Since all the other tables were taken, begrudgingly, he allowed the inquisitors to be seated there.

"These awful men," Abby hissed to Jacob once they were settled.

"They are no worse than the wits," he hissed back.

"At least the wits have humour, albeit withering. These politicians are…" Noticing Thackery's boy approaching with the coffee pot, she fell silent.

"Is there chocolate, lad?" Jacob asked.

"Nay, sir, only coffee," the child replied, adding woodenly, "However 'tis the best coffee in all of London."

Having poured two bowls of the steaming brew, the boy held out his hand. "One penny each, sir."

When Jacob dipped into his pouch, a look of puzzlement crossed his face. When he retrieved his hand, it was filled with coins - clearly more than he had anticipated. Except… On closer inspection, he saw that many were not coins at all.

"From the alcove in the…" he began to exclaim, wisely stopping himself. In a calmer tone, he asked Abby, "What are they?"

The boy picked one out and held it up. In relief on the pewter disc were the words 'Union in Cornhill' and the number '3'. "'Tis an old coffee house token, sir," he explained. "Gentlemen purchase them from the proprietor and use them in place of coins. This one is from The Union coffee house in Cornhill, which burned down. And here," he picked out a smaller copper token, "The

Chapter Coffee House in Paternoster Row. This one," he selected another, "is from Pasqua Rosée's…"

"Aye, lad, enough," Jacob interjected, snapping his hand shut.

"None may be used here, sir," the boy continued undaunted. "You would require a token from The Gilded Bean coffee house on St Martin's…"

Jacob clipped him round the ear and sent him on his way with two penny coins. "Why would these old coffee-house tokens be in that alcove?" he asked Abby.

She put a finger to her lips. "We should discourse when we're alone," she replied. "We're here for the trap-door."

"Should we both investigate?" he asked, glancing towards the door behind Thomas Thackery.

"It would appear suspicious. You must go."

Jacob was unsure whether to whistle or perhaps saunter as he made his way past Thackery's counter. The proprietor's eyes, he noticed, were monitoring his progress, and it made him feel still more self-conscious. *Should I wave?* he wondered.

Distracted by such thoughts, he tripped over a chair leg and fell into a seated Member of Parliament. The blustering fellow pushed him away angrily, and Jacob righted his skewed periwig while grinning inanely at Thackery. The proprietor scowled back.

Jacob saw that Abby had her head in her hands.

Opening the back door, he took one last glance at Thackery, who was still eyeing him intently, and slipped inside, closing the door behind him.

The din from the coffee house was muffled here, and he looked around.

He was in what appeared to be a store-room, some twenty-five feet square. To his right was a door, behind which his nose told him was the privy. A few dozen kilderkin barrels, each around 18 inches high, were piled in the corner to his left, and beside them were several sacks and wooden crates stacked against the wall.

The boarded floor beyond the crates was hidden from view. When he moved closer, he saw it straight away: the trap-door.

Jacob felt a shiver down his spine.

Standing over the trap-door, he saw that the wood was worn and scuffed, with heavy iron hinges and a large bolt beside an iron lifting ring, which were all rusted. The gaps all around the four sides were filled with detritus; it made him wonder whether the door had not been used in a while.

"There is but one way to find out," he told himself.

Clasping the bolt handle with his index and middle fingers, he tugged.

It did not budge.

He tried again, harder.

Nothing.

Cursing to himself, he went looking for a tool to help force the corroded metalwork and was buoyed to find a hammer among the assorted tools in the first crate he inspected.

Returning to the bolt, he hit the handle hard with the hammer.

It moved, albeit accompanied by a loud *donk*.

Checking the back door and seeing it closed, Jacob threw caution to the wind and hit the bolt several times in succession - *donk-donk-donk-donk* - until it was freed from its iron clasp.

Still no one came to investigate.

Taking the lifting ring in both hands and bracing his feet on either side of the trap-door, Jacob pulled upwards with all his strength.

"May I assist you?"

Jacob let the ring fall back and harrumphed. "I was…"

"I can see what you were doin'," interjected Thackery, closing the back door behind him. "That hatch does not open."

"Aye," Jacob replied, brushing at his collar.

"I can't help but wonder why you'd wish to open it." Without waiting for a reply, Thackery went on, "I've owned The Gilded Bean since 1658. In all them intervening years, that trap-door has remained immovable. I was told it leads to Rose's Coffee House on The Strand.

However, since I can walk there on St Martin's Lane in barely a moment, I've never felt the need to force it."

Jacob adjusted his periwig.

Thackery smiled. "Were you requiring the privy, sir?"

"How went it?" Abby asked eagerly when Jacob returned to their table.

"We should leave," he told her under his breath.

Seeing that he meant it, she rose from her chair and followed him towards the exit.

"You have not drunk your coffee!" the proprietor called after them, the hint of a smirk in his tone.

Jacob turned around. "Aye, 'tis cold," he replied.

"You, sir!"

What now? thought Jacob, turning to find Clement Culpepper pointing in his direction. "Me, sir?"

"Aye, you, sir. Pray, be seated. I wish to hear more of your Mr Pepys." Culpepper noticed Jacob glance warily towards Abby, and added exasperatedly, "She may accompany you, however I expect to hear not a peep from her dainty little mouth."

Chapter Fifteen

The Armitage Company

Guy Kelburne was intrigued to have found a link to his uncle. He visited the young woman who had spoken to him while he was detained in Knaresborough's stocks.

Her name was Ursula, and she was the daughter of Gunpowder Treason Plot conspirator Thomas Winter. She was born in 1606, a few months after her father met the same fate as Guy Fawkes. Fearing further retribution, her grandmother, Jane Gresham, had whisked the infant Ursula and her siblings far from London to the family estate outside Knaresborough known as Armitage Court.

Guy had never seen the like of such a grand old manor house, accessed via an ancient gatehouse and set among lawns and gardens that stretched as far as the eye could see. When he entered the house for the first time, Ursula watched amused as his eyes travelled up and around, marvelling at the rich tapestries and austere portraiture, the suspended chandeliers and delicate ornaments.

Jane Gresham's husband had died some years ago, leaving the wizened matriarch in charge, and she seemed to delight in collecting young folk around her. Besides Ursula's siblings – brothers Bertram and Percival, and sister Dorcas Langley (who was in mourning, her husband, Nicholas Langley, who had lately succumbed to dropsy) – the distant wings of the house played host to a revolving cast of waifs and strays.

Having learned of the incident at Knaresborough – the final straw – Henry Kelburne dismissed his youngest, wayward son from the family home in Scotton. Subsequently, Guy was welcomed into Armitage Court as another of those darling strays.

Although the family was cosseted within thick stone walls, 200 miles from King James and the royal court, talk of the Gunpowder Treason Plot was frowned upon and discussed only rarely, in hushed voices. "Be wary, Guy, for the very walls have ears," Jane told her new young charge.

It was why, she explained, she employed no servants, and the residents were responsible for the running of the household. Guy took over the baking of the bread, having helped his mother with the same using his father's freshly milled flour, and he introduced cock ale to the others, having purloined his mother's secret recipe.

Money appeared to be no object, and life felt idyllic, although there were occasional glimpses of lingering unease in the mind of the matriarch.

Everyone dutifully attended Anglican services at the local church, in contrast to their Catholic heritage, and for several months Anne welcomed into the house a disfigured, scowling man who arrived with a cart-load of swords hidden beneath hay.

Known only as Ralph, he was said to be a relative who had fought on the side of the Spanish Catholics against the Protestant Dutch in the Eighty Years War. Ralph tutored all the young men of Armitage Court in the art of sword-fighting.

It felt as though Jane was preparing her own private army, which led to a sense of unease that no one voiced.

Meanwhile, as they grew to know one another, seated in a semi-circle around a fireplace deep into the night, Guy found himself falling for Ursula, and she for him.

To amuse themselves, the young residents formed an amateur theatre company, which they named The Armitage Company. Taking it in turns as actors and audience, they would perform for the matriarch.

The plays of William Shakespeare, who had died less than a decade ago, were among their favourites. Shakespeare's work had become celebrated during his lifetime, and Ursula and her siblings had been treated to early performances of 'Hamlet', 'The Merchant of Venice' and 'Romeo & Juliet' in York, which they recreated - crudely, if with great enthusiasm - at Armitage Court.

Where men of the day traditionally played female roles in the professional theatre, within the anarchic confines of the manor house there were no such constraints. Which is how Ursula came to play Juliet opposite Guy's Romeo, and they first stole a kiss that was meant to be staged, to the delight of the spectators.

Guy was, by a distance, the most gifted actor present. His predilection for showing off, and his naturally gregarious manner, meant that he was devoid of the self-consciousness that blighted so many of the other performers. When he donned a costume, he became the character. He embodied the role, and he believed in himself.

Indeed, so self-assured was he that he indulged in an experiment. Without Jane's knowledge, since he felt sure she would put a stop to it, he dressed himself in one of her late husband's most extravagant outfits and walked into Knaresborough. There, he strolled self-importantly about the town, watched surreptitiously by Ursula and other Armitage players, until he came upon the constable who had so publicly humiliated him in the stocks.

Declaring himself to be an envoy for the newly installed King, he spun a tale concerning a potential royal visit, so eloquently and with such arrogant conviction that the bamboozled official was entirely taken in.

The same group and Guy, relieved of his disguise, returned to Knaresborough that night. They watched, hidden from view, as a succession of dignitaries bearing gifts made their way to the Town Hall. Ushered inside by the constable, they expected to encounter the King's envoy for a meeting they hoped would endow royal patronage upon their businesses.

As the night wore on, the dignitaries spilled out of the hall in dribs and drabs, in varying states of outrage, while the constable waved his arms and blustered excuses.

The resounding success of Guy's subversion only increased his already boundless confidence, and he suggested that the Armitage Company begin writing their own material.

Alas, Guy proved to be no satirical playwright. Fortuitously, while his verse was hackneyed, there were others in the troupe - Ursula among them - who were more proficient, and could rewrite his work behind the scenes, allowing him to take the credit.

One of these early plays was entitled 'The Crowning of the King, Or England's Shameful Folly'. It drew gasps when he announced it, and there was unanimous disapproval in the aftermath. A few of the troupe left the drawing room in disgust; two of the newer members, brothers Reuben and Miles Wakefield, were so appalled by such a blatant act of sedition that they left the house altogether.

Later, such were Guy's conviction and allure that he was able to turn the core family members to his way of thinking. "A fire of rebellion still burns in your grandmother's heart," he told them. "I can sense it." When they looked unconvinced, he added, "We shall perform the play behind locked doors, to Jane alone, and she will adore it, I promise you."

Thus, one warm spring night in 1627, the bare bones of the Armitage Company debuted their production of 'The Crowning of the King, Or England's Shameful Folly' at Armitage Court. Secretly, Guy hoped that it would meet with his host's approval and lead to similar productions, which they might even take on the road, to perform in the top rooms of inns to carefully selected audiences. Such wanton audacity appealed to him.

However, the play did not meet with Jane Gresham's approval. On the contrary, she was horrified.

A mere quarter of an hour in, with the full madness of the production revealed, she rose angrily from her armchair to put a halt to the proceedings. In the same instant, the main door to the manor house could be heard crashing inward, accompanied by the shouts of angry men.

One of the voices they recognised as Reuben Wakefield's.

Guy stared at Ursula in alarm; she shook her head at him, grim-faced.

"Hurry, make your escape!" Jane urged, pointing at the rear door of the drawing room. "I shall hold them off," she added, hobbling as fast as she could towards the main door.

Guy was the first through the rear door, imploring the others to hurry. Ursula's brothers and sister made it through, but she was laden down with a costume made of so many petticoats.

As Ursula tripped and fell, the main drawing room door flew off its hinges, sending Jane, who was braced against it, careering backwards.

Guy slammed their door shut and wrestled with Dorcas and her brothers, who tried to stop him from turning the key.

"'Tis them or us!" he told them, wild-eyed.

The family members had planned for the day when they were hunted by the King's men and had a safe house already in mind. However, in the darkness and panic, Guy became separated from the others, subsequently finding himself alone and in hiding.

When news reached him of the executions of Jane and Ursula, it made up his mind for him.

He would travel to London incognito. There, he would assume a new identity. He could be anybody he wanted to be, he had already proved that to himself.

And he would bide his time.

Chapter Sixteen

The Bill

Culpepper and his stocky companion, whom he introduced as Jasper Davenport - "We are Members of *Parliament!*" he told the inquisitors, enunciating each syllable with relish - were sitting beside one another at a round table, leaving Abby and Jacob to take two chairs opposite.

Culpepper summoned the coffee-boy and ordered that he charge the inquisitors' bowls. They did not dare demur, but stared gloomily as the levels of murky brew rose before them.

"Pray tell, sir, how is my good friend, Mr Pepys?" the MP asked in his nasal voice, retrieving a copy of the subscription-only *London Gazette* newspaper from his table.

"You know him, sir?" Jacob replied, still gazing in horror at his coffee.

"He does not," Davenport interjected, sucking on his clay pipe. "However, he is aware that Pepys has the King's ear."

Culpepper swiped limply at his companion's cheek. "Ignore this clodpate, Mr… I did not catch the name?"

"I am Jacob Standish, sir. This is…"

"And you are Mr Pepys's *inquisitor*? Pray, what is your purpose, sir?"

Abby supped at length from her coffee bowl, although she hated the drink, purely to hide her facial expression from the dreadful old men. Culpepper, she decided, looked like a weasel, and Davenport, a toad. *The weasel and the toad*, she thought to herself with satisfaction, blotting out their discourse.

"We investigate crimes," Jacob explained, and he went on to outline their recent cases. It became quickly apparent to him that neither MP was listening. Culpepper was engrossed in something on the front page of the *Gazette*, while Davenport began conversing with a gentleman at the table behind.

"Hmm, hmm, most edifying," Culpepper muttered.

Jacob stopped talking mid-sentence. Neither MP noticed.

Culpepper nudged his companion, who paid him no heed whatsoever. "'Tis such a delight, Jasper, to sup here for a penny, suck on a tobacco pipe, and have all the news of this fair city laid before me gratis. It never ceases to amaze me."

Davenport remained deep in conversation with the gentleman behind, concerning the King's response to the recent fire.

"Mr Culpepper?" piped up Abby.

"Oh!" the startled MP exclaimed.

"What can you tell us about the King's Public Order & Safety Bill?"

Culpepper fanned himself vigorously, as if about to faint.

Turning away from his conversation, Davenport leaned across the table, his face in Abby's. His plump, flushed cheeks glistened greasily.

"If I did hand to you the very Bill," he said slowly, all coffee-breath and tobacco smoke, "you would not be able to read it."

"Try me, sir," she said, avoiding his beady stare.

Without taking his eyes off her, he reached to his left and pulled a handbill from the wall.

Abby took it from him and read it aloud.

The Public Order & Safety Bill
Pertaining to Public Houses
A Bill proposing the regulation of public houses, including coffee houses, inns, taverns, and alehouses, which have become venues for disorderly conduct and activities which may compromise Public Order and Safety.

Regulation of Public Assemblies

No public house shall permit gatherings exceeding a specified number of patrons at any given time without prior approval from the Local Authority. A record of attendees must be presented upon request by said Authority to ensure Public Order.

Control of Printed Materials

It shall be required that all printed or written materials displayed or distributed within a public house do adhere to strict standards of Public Decency as defined by the Local Authority.

Surveillance

Public houses will be subject to regular inspections by appointed Officials to ensure compliance with all Regulations in order to safeguard Public Safety.

Penalties

Violation of any Provision of this Act shall result in fines, imprisonment, or both, as deemed appropriate by the Local Authority.

This Bill is Proposed by His Most Excellent Majesty King Charles II, with the Counsel and Consent of the esteemed Members of Parliament, Clement Culpepper and Jasper Davenport.

Folding the handbill, she gave it to Jacob, who placed it in his satchel.

Davenport harrumphed lustily. "You can read," he said with barely disguised contempt.

"My father taught me, sir," she replied. "He was a printer."

"A printer!" Davenport exploded. "The very bane of our society! Scurrilous blackguards churning out nought but seditious drivel, spewing forth lies, dissent and more lies. I would flog them all! They hide behind their presses, undermining the very fabric…" The riled MP dissolved into a fit of wheezing and coughing, such that Culpepper had to slap him heartily on the back.

Still slapping, Culpepper addressed Jacob. "You will mention me to Mr Pepys, won't you? Clement Culpepper. Member of Parliament for Winchester."

His colleague managed to suppress his choking just long enough to blurt out, "And Jasper Davenport!"

"Aye, sirs," Jacob replied, somewhat taken aback. "I will be sure to."

Culpepper smiled to himself and abandoned his attempts at resuscitating Davenport, who dropped to his knees, heaving.

"Mr Culpepper?" said Abby.

The MP wrinkled his nose at her. "If you must," he sniffed.

"This Bill you propose… Is it popular?"

Culpepper straightened, pulling his coat tight around him. "What is your point?"

"I imagine your reputation rests upon it, sir."

Culpepper's eyes blazed. "Insolent girl! Do you question my authority?"

Abby's cheeks flushed. "Nay, sir, I would never countenance such a thing."

Jacob spoke up. "I believe what my fellow inquisitor is asking is…" He halted, flummoxed.

Davenport, finally able to retake his seat, purple-faced, finished the sentence for him. "Is the Bill contentious?"

No one spoke.

"Indeed it is contentious! Mighty contentious!" Davenport bellowed, causing several other patrons to turn and stare. "What use would it be were it not so?"

"There are… elements," Culpepper cut in, "who would prefer to see it fail. I will see them buried in the ground."

Davenport slammed a fist onto the table. "*If we can prove their treachery, Clement.* Only through unwavering vigilance and decisive action can we ensure the safety and stability of our realm."

Culpepper patted his hand. "And that is why I take decisive action, Jasper."

Davenport whipped his hand away and glowered at Culpepper. "Then keep your agents in line, sir," he growled. "For they feed you nought but scraps. I will not see my reputation sullied by your incompetence."

Culpepper laughed nervously, nodding unsubtly in Jacob's direction. "Do not forget, Jasper, that we have a guest."

"*Guests*, Clement, *guests*. For *she*," Davenport pointed angrily at Abby, "is more dangerous than *he*." Leering at her, spittle on his lips, he added, "Are you not, my dear?"

Abby shrank back in her seat.

Jacob deftly changed the subject. "You are both patrons of the Arts, I believe?"

Davenport peered at him suspiciously. "Who told you so?"

Culpepper let out a high-pitched laugh. "He refers to the Exalted Competition of the Arts, which we did sponsor, Jasper. Do you not, sir?"

Jacob nodded, picked up his coffee, and drained it in one.

Davenport leant in towards the inquisitors and spoke deliberately, glaring from one to the other. "When Banqueting Hall is filled with men of power and learning, we will read the Bill, with the King by our side. Then they will support it." He pulled back and added sharply, "Now begone. I tire of you both."

The inquisitors needed no further bidding.

As Jacob stepped towards the door, exhaling quietly through puffed cheeks, Culpepper called to him. "What did you say your name was?"

"Standish, sir. Jacob Standish."

The MP regarded him quizzically. "Are you related to Sir Miles Standish?"

"Indeed I am, sir. He was my father."

The MPs exchanged glances. Davenport scowled and shooed them away, as one might dismiss a dog.

Chapter Seventeen

Return to Jacob's

The inquisitors ran down St Martin's Lane and onto The Strand, only stopping when they had put sufficient distance between themselves and The Gilded Bean. They found themselves in the grand doorway of a five-storey stone-built mansion, with Roman pillars on either side. Gentlemen and ladies wafted past, sporting the latest fashions: a lace parasol in her hand, a waist-high gold-topped cane in his.

"Jacob, they're using the Arts challenge to push through their Bill!" Abby said, catching her breath. "They have no interest in poetry."

He mopped his brow. "Did they murder Eustace? What was it that Culpepper said?"

"He said, 'I will see them in the ground.'"

"Aye. And I would believe it possible."

Abby pushed a wavy red strand of hair from her eye. "They wouldn't do the deed themselves. They wouldn't dare. Nor sully their finely manicured hands."

"There was talk of agents…"

"Aye, but the trap-door does not open, so how would such an agent gain access to Rose's from The Gilded Bean?"

Her fellow inquisitor shook his head.

"There are rum goings-on here, Jacob, in the monied end of London. I almost wish we were back in Deptford."

He shuddered at the memory. All those reminders of his failed career; all those seafaring men laughing at the pampered son of Sir Miles Standish. "What do these wits and MPs know of my father that I do not?" he asked. "First Vincent's innuendo, then Culpepper and Davenport, exchanging furtive glances. What does it mean? Did I not know my father?"

"Hush, Jacob, we should return to your house where we may discourse in private." Abby looked around her, catching the eye of a passing hackney coachman, who winked at her. "I feel unsafe here."

On their way back to Strand Lane, Abby showed Jacob the market on Holywell Street. They found a cookshop selling beef, mutton, veal and lamb off the spit, served in a bread roll with salt and mustard. Both asked for theirs to be sliced with the fat on, and walked away chewing contentedly, famished after their mental exertions.

Having finished off the meal in Jacob's dining room, washed down with ale, Abby pulled out her quill and notebook to list their suspects. Noting that a link existed between the two coffee houses, albeit that the route seemed blocked, she included those from The Gilded Bean on her list.

Rose Trewin - proprietor of Rose's Coffee House
Rupert Mortimer - wit
Vincent Mortimer - wit
Zebulon Strangeway - quack physician
Thomas Thackery - proprietor of The Gilded Bean coffee house
Clement Culpepper - MP
Jasper Davenport - MP

"Do we add Quigley?" she asked.
Jacob nearly fell off his stool.

James Quigley - coney-catcher

Jacob took a gulp of ale. "'Tis a lengthy list," he said, licking his lips.

Abby savoured the feel of the quill. "Eight," she said. "What would be their reasons for murdering Eustace?"

"Everybody loathed the pompous oaf!"

"Aye, 'tis true." Abby sighed. "Then there's the rivalry for the King's Arts Challenge. The prize money - fifty

guineas – is sufficient to drive any immoral man to
murder."

"Blount was opposed to the King, I am sure. Indeed,
I believe Rose's to be a hotbed of parliamentarian
sympathies. Thus Culpepper and Davenport may have
targeted him."

"Yet we found no passable route from The Gilded
Bean to Rose's when her doors are locked."

"What if somebody picked the locks?"

Abby threw her arms in the air. "Why did you not
suggest that sooner?"

"It only just occurred to me," he replied sulkily, straightening his periwig. "It would implicate
Quigley," he added.

"Jacob, the old man's a thief, not a murderer."

"Then what of the quack, Strangeway?"

"He too appears harmless."

Jacob snorted. "Not to me! There was blood on his
dagger! The man is a charlatan of the lowest order. I
would trust him no more than I would trust the knave
Quigley."

"What of our proprietors, Rose and Thackery?"

"The woman has secrets." When Abby nodded
in agreement, he continued, "And Thackery..." He
laughed wryly. "He seems too stupid for skulldug-
gery."

"Nevertheless, we should investigate them both."

"I would investigate Quigley first," Jacob replied. "He troubles me."

There came a sharp rapping on the front door. The inquisitors stiffened and stared at one another. Instinctively, Abby rose to answer it, but Jacob motioned for her to sit.

"Who could it be?" she asked. "Do you expect guests?"

"I never expect guests," he told her, heading for the door.

A hunched old man was on the doorstep, wearing a long black cassock with a white clerical collar, clutching a walking stick in his shaking hand. In the other was a Holy Bible.

His head was bowed, and a wide-brimmed black hat covered much of his face, but Jacob could see that he had a tatty grey beard and pale, dry lips. A worn leather satchel sat at his feet, containing what looked to be religious pamphlets.

"Good day to you, sir," he said, in a thin, quavering voice. "I am Father William Arbuthnot."

When Jacob said nothing, only stared, he continued, "I represent the charity Children After the Fire, sir. Here is my letter of authority from the bishop himself." With a trembling hand, the priest placed his Bible on the ground, selected a folded sheet of paper from his bag, and handed it over.

Jacob read the letter perfunctorily, not sure what he was looking for, saw that it was indeed signed by The Right Reverend Bishop of London, Humphrey Henchman, and handed it back. "What is your purpose at my door?" he asked, praying the old man would not ask for money.

"I seek donations, sir. Many thousands of children have been rendered homeless by the terrible fire that swept through London. A small donation would provide for one poor soul a warm meal and accommodation for the night."

Jacob patted around his waist, taking care not to jingle his money pouch. "I fear, father, that my coins are all gone."

"A grander donation would provide for two or more children," the priest persisted. "Perhaps you have some money inside the house?" He gazed upward. "It is indeed a mighty fine house."

Abby appeared beside Jacob and the priest lowered his head. "May I assist you, Mr Quigley?" she asked, removing his hat.

Before Jacob's widening eyes, the 'priest' stood bolt upright, cast aside the walking stick, peeled off his beard and grinned at him as if they were long-lost friends.

"Quigley!" he roared, outraged, and launched himself at the terrible old man.

While Jacob simmered in an armchair at the far end of the parlour, Abby handed Quigley an ale as he warmed his feet by the fire.

"I wouldn't have taken your money," the old coney-catcher called across to Jacob. "I was merely playing. Force of habit."

Abby took a seat beside him. "Come, join us, Jacob," she said.

Jacob, however, would not be cajoled.

"Were you aware that Jacob lived here?" Abby asked Quigley, savouring her own claret - a drink she could never have afforded.

"Indeed," he replied. "I know every address in Westminster. I make it my business."

"Then why did you come here? If not to fleece my friend?"

Across the room, Jacob's ears pricked up. *Did she refer to me as a friend?* he thought. Colleagues, they had been, but friends? *I suppose we are*, he considered, nodding cheerfully to himself.

"I thought you might need some assistance," Quigley replied. "We had a deal, after all."

Jacob pulled up a chair beside Abby. "What can you tell us about Rose?" he asked the old coney-catcher.

"Ha!" Quigley exclaimed, patting his own knee several times. "It all depends upon what you wish to know, Mr

Standish, and whether you can discern fact from fiction. For rumour follows her like a lamb follows its mother."

"I must warn you," he began, "that Rose's opened some eight years ago, and time mists the telling of its story. You would hear ten different tales from ten other men. Mine," he brushed imaginary dust off his cassock, "is the finest."

It went like this...

Rose arrived in Westminster in 1658, two years before Quigley moved to London from Bristol - where, coincidentally, the port authorities had just clamped down on petty crime - to "seek his fortune". Some said she came from the south coast; others, from Cambridgeshire; others, from the wilds of Cornwall. No one could agree.

"Why do you not simply ask her?" Jacob suggested.

"I have done so. On several occasions. She gives a different answer each time."

Her basement premises, on the corner of the increasingly fashionable Strand and St Martin's Lane, were, at the time of her purchase, a disreputable alehouse. Inspired by the tales of Pasqua Rosée's first London coffee house becoming an instant success, Rose decided to do away with the alcohol and sell coffee.

Rumour had it that the original Rose's - if only briefly - was frequented by local Members of Parliament, attracted from the nearby Palace of Westminster, where they conducted their duties.

"Why briefly?" Abby asked.

"The Gilded Bean also opened," said Quigley.

Thomas Thackery appeared in Westminster, he explained, either shortly before Rose or shortly afterwards. None could agree on the timings. Either way, Thackery opened The Gilded Bean behind her establishment, and, within days, its luxurious interior had enticed away the MPs. She was left with the wits, who seemed to equate the squalor of her basement establishment with their exhausting yet ultimately heroic toil with a quill.

Jacob moved his chair closer to the fire. "Was there animosity betwixt she and Thackery?"

"Not as I am aware," Quigley replied. "I heard they were acquainted for a brief while. Never have I seen them together myself."

"A most engaging story," said Abby, applauding lightly.

Quigley raised a gold-ringed finger. "Ah, but there is more. There exists another telling of said tale, in which the coffee house was opened not by Rose, but by Pasqua Rosée himself. Yet it was under his stewardship so fleetingly that many knew nought of him, or else believed the tale to be nonsense, concocted to undermine the woman."

"Surely certain Members of Parliament at The Gilded Bean would recall those days?" Abby asked. "Why not enquire there?"

"Many new MPs arrived in 1660, when the King returned, replacing those from the days of the Rump Parliament. But, aye, a good number remained in place, and some of those would frequent The Gilded Bean. However, I would never ask a question of a Member of Parliament."

"Why not?" asked Jacob.

"Since a more mendacious, cheating, conniving group of scoundrels would be hard to find, sir. Why, I would rather trust…"

"Yourself?" Jacob suggested.

"I'd prefer 'a common thief', sir."

The coal fire had died down, and Abby prodded it with a brass poker, sparking it back to life. "Mr Quigley?" she said. "Am I able to see Eustace Blount's body? His bruising irks me."

"As you are well aware, mistress, I know nought of this body of which you speak." He continued before she could interject, "However, were I to guess as to its whereabouts, I would imagine that it is floating down the Thames."

As he departed, seeing himself out, Quigley called back, "I almost omitted to mention. Thackery's coffee-boy. I've seen him lurk discreetly 'twixt the two coffee houses."

Chapter Eighteen

Traitor's Gate

They turned in early. The inquisitors breakfasted on cold meats and were out of the house just as the neighbouring church bells chimed seven, one shortly after the other. The dissonance echoed pleasingly in the morning air.

"I dreamed of my father," Jacob told her as he locked the front door. "He was the size of a giant, and I sat on his shoulder as he bestrode the land. Behind us, tall oak trees grew in his footsteps."

Abby wrinkled her nose. "You hold him in high esteem."

London was rousing from its slumber – not that the great city ever truly slept. A high wind during the night had cleared the persistent smog, revealing a grey and watery morning sky. The sooty pall would soon return.

A pig nearly bowled Jacob over as it was herded into one of the butcher's shops behind the towering maypole. "Foul creature," he muttered.

"Do you think your father concealed something from you?" Abby asked as they continued along The Strand towards the coffee houses.

Jacob stopped. "I find it inconceivable," he said. 'He was one of the King's most trusted allies."

She stopped too. "Was he not a republican during the time of Cromwell's Commonwealth?"

Although it was an innocent question, Jacob rounded on her angrily. "Many good men changed their allegiance," he snapped, "once they saw that the King's desires for his people were right and proper. His Majesty made my father his right-hand man. He entrusted him to hunt down the ringleaders of the plot against his own father, and rewarded him well when he succeeded.

"That fine house in which I reside was once owned by Sir William Pride, who signed the death warrant of King Charles I."

"What happened to Pride?" Abby asked.

"He rests on a spike at Traitor's Gate."

Outside the door to Rose's Coffee House, Abby and Jacob were discussing their plan of action when a familiar nasal voice came from behind them.

"Only the fool speculates, Mr Standish!"

It was Clement Culpepper, crossing The Strand in the direction of St Martin's Lane. His velvet coat was royal blue, and he swung his cane gaily, as if performing on stage.

"Sir!" said Jacob, waving for him to stop. "Concerning my father…"

Culpepper sauntered past with nary a glance in Jacob's direction. "Busy, busy!" he called out in a sing-song voice.

Jacob glared at his receding back. "Busy drinking coffee," he muttered.

Abby, he noticed, was tugging his sleeve. "What is it?" he asked.

"Did you hear what he said?" she hissed.

"Aye. Busy, busy'." He tutted.

"Before that."

Jacob shook his head.

"He said, 'Only the fool speculates' – that's what I say to you, Jacob. I said it to you yesterday."

"Aye, I recall it."

"But he wasn't present when I did so. Somebody related our discourse to him."

Jacob squinted. "A spy?"

"Aye," she replied. "I'm sure of it."

"What if Culpepper also uses the phrase, 'Only the fool speculates'? It is not yours to keep."

Abby sighed, exasperated. "Those are my words, Jacob."

Chapter Nineteen

A Poem

Rupert Mortimer was reciting a love poem, prancing from foot to foot, when Rose opened the basement door to the inquisitors. The instant he saw them, he sat down and folded his arms sulkily. "I would not waste *mes mots exquisite* upon them; 'twould cast pearls before swine!" he told his audience, which consisted solely of his brother.

The coffee was already brewing. The aroma was so potent, the inquisitors could almost taste it, and they were not yet overpowered by the great clouds of tobacco smoke that would eventually choke the space like a thick London fog.

"May we join you?" Abby asked, taking a seat before either wit could reply. Apologetically, Jacob pulled up a stool beside her.

Rupert waved a hankie beneath his nose. "What an awful smell."

"Aye," said Abby. "'Tis your poetry. It lingers in the air like a foul miasma."

Vincent found the quip delightful, Rupert less so, and the two brothers began scuffling. Arriving with two bowls for the new customers, Rose regarded the wits with an air of matronly resignation.

Jacob lifted his bowl, sniffed the contents, and took a tentative sip.

"What's the matter?" Abby asked.

"Chocolate," he hissed.

"Ah! She admires you!"

Jacob grimaced. "I fear I have developed a taste for the coffee drink."

Getting straight to work, Abby asked the Mortimers, "Who are John Fryer and Henry Corbet?"

The brothers eyed her warily, puffing on their clay pipes. "From whom did you hear those names?" Vincent asked.

"Sir, we are Mr Samuel Pepys's personal inquisitors," Jacob replied. "It is our business."

Vincent blew on his steaming coffee. "Then you yourself will doubtless tell us who they are."

Pulling the 'Citizens, Arise!' handbill from her satchel, the one the inquisitors had found in the secret printing room, Abby placed it on the table.

Vincent snatched it up and ripped it to shreds. "Where did you find it?" he demanded. "You play a dangerous game."

Abby glanced across at Rose, grinding beans with her pestle and mortar, aware she was listening in. "Good sirs, we are unconcerned with your politics..." Seeing that Jacob was poised to interject, she kicked him under the table. "We wish only to discover who murdered your colleague, Eustace Blount."

No one spoke. A drip of dirty water fell from the ceiling, narrowly missing Abby's chocolate. Rupert looked to Vincent, who pursed his lips.

Seeing that a stand-off had developed, Abby took the lead. "John Fryer and Henry Corbet were your fellow wits, who were engaged in printing seditious pamphlets challenging the King's sovereignty. One day, they didn't join you at Rose's, even though you expected them. Later you discovered they'd been arrested and imprisoned."

Vincent Mortimer sipped his coffee, staring at her over the brim of the bowl.

"Were they executed?" Abby asked.

Rupert could contain himself no longer. "How do you know all this? Who told you?"

Jacob reached into his own bag, retrieved a handbill, and gave it to the wit.

"'Zebulon Strangeway's Miracle Tonic'?" Rupert spluttered. "'Restore your vitality'? What balderdash is this?"

"I do beg your pardon," Jacob exclaimed. "'Tis the wrong handbill."

Rooting around some more, he produced the correct piece of paper.

Vincent read it and sneered. "The accursed Public Order & Safety Bill. It concerns not public order but the King's control. It is censorship writ large."

"Hush, brother!" Rupert urged.

Jacob rested his elbows on the table. "Have you opened the trap-door that leads to The Gilded Bean?"

Vincent exhaled a cloud of pipe smoke. "I know not of what you speak."

Rupert sighed. "The trap-door is old and disused. It does not operate. We have tried and failed."

"Who murdered Eustace?" Abby asked.

The Mortimers looked at one another.

"You are the lofty inquisitors," Rupert replied. "We are merely extravagantly gifted wits."

"Aye, you tell us," his brother added.

Rupert rose from his stool, bowed towards the inquisitors, and improvised a poem.

Oh noble inquisitors,
So wise and so grand,

Your minds are so sharp,
Yet your judgements so bland.

Wiping an imaginary tear from his eye, he continued.

Your questions so pointed,
You prod and you pry,
Yet all you'll uncover,
Is a fresh web of lies.

Bowing once again, he disappeared towards the privy, applauded loudly by his brother.

"That put us in our place," Abby told Jacob, who was furiously adjusting his periwig.

Chapter Twenty

Rose's Story

The proprietor called the inquisitors over. Her black hair was untied and fell down her back; she wore a silk, boned bodice that tapered at the waist and a crimson gown with lace edging. Even in the half-light of the coffee house, her whole being shimmered.

She was sitting forward in her armchair, pounding her roasted coffee beans into a grit. Behind her, on the floor, Jacob noticed an open sack of green beans.

"The raw coffee beans, Mr Standish," she told him. "They turn brown when roasted over a fire. 'Tis a tiresome process, making coffee for these ludicrous popinjays."

"You do not respect their talents?" Jacob asked.

"Which talents would those be?"

"You don't believe they'll win the King's 50 guineas?" Abby asked.

Rose laid down her pestle. "Eustace stood perhaps a chance. The Mortimers pen pure drivel." Seeing that

Abby and Jacob were standing awkwardly, she told them, "Fetch stools. We must discourse further."

"You wear expensive clothing and keep an enviable library," Abby noted, nodding towards the proprietor's bookshelf.

"They're gifts," she replied. "From suitors."

"The wits?" Jacob asked.

Rose snorted so loudly that even the Mortimers were drawn momentarily from their self-absorption. "They adore me," she replied. "They shower me with cheap trinkets I cast into the remains of the River Tyburn."

"Who gave you *Leviathan*?" Abby asked, knowing it to be beyond a wit's means.

Rose stopped pounding her beans. "'Tis a private matter."

"We spoke with Jim Quigley," Abby added.

"A reliable source. What did he say of me?"

"He told us he knows not even from whence you hail," Jacob replied. "That your tales change with the seasons."

"Would you wish me to tell you?"

Rose explained that she was born in 1618 in Fowey, Cornwall. "Trewin is a fine Cornish name." Her household was humble; her father worked as a blacksmith and her mother as a washerwoman. As a young girl, she would sweep the forge and help sort the laundry into different fabrics.

The winters were harsh, she said, and Fowey, a strategic deep-river port on the English Channel, could be a windswept place. She had five siblings – two sisters and three brothers, all younger – and often they would starve, relying on the local community for scraps.

Neither her sister nor her youngest brother survived childhood; as the eldest sibling, she felt responsible.

When she was old enough, Rose began a career as a seamstress, having become accustomed to fabrics and the composition of garments. She also began to spin and weave her own wool. It was a living of sorts and helped contribute to the family's meagre income.

Everything changed when England went to war with itself. Cornwall was staunchly royalist, and her brothers, Gideon and Peregrine, aged 21 and 19, signed up to fight for King Charles when the Civil War broke out in 1642.

The first major battle on Cornish soil occurred the following year. Her brothers, under the leadership of Sir Ralph Hopton, helped capture almost 1,500 parliamentarian troops at Braddock Down. Their opponents fired barely a shot, so swift had been the royalist charge.

The Cornish royalists then pushed eastwards into Devon, until an army of 8,000 under Robert Devereaux, 3rd Earl of Essex, forced them back across the River Tamar. On learning that a royalist army was advancing on his rearguard, Essex had no choice but to press further into Cornwall.

News reached Rose's family that the parliamentarian army was heading for Fowey, with plans to evacuate by sea. "I remember it as though it were yesterday," she said. "My father urged me to flee, to follow the cliffs to Readymoney Cove and hide there. I begged him to join me, but he vowed to defend our home. My mother stayed with him. It was the last I saw of them."

After the cannon smoke had cleared, 6,000 parliamentarian infantrymen had surrendered, and Gabriel and Peregrine lay dead on a battlefield beside the ruins of Restormel Castle, some seven miles from where they were born.

"You must have hated Cromwell," Abby said.

Rose's nostrils flared. "I reserved my hatred for the King. 'Twas his greed for power that ignited the war. But for him, my parents and brothers would be alive."

Orphaned and alone, she walked to London in September 1645 with no more plan than to start a new life. Her journey took two weeks. The weather was atrocious, her shoes fell apart, and she arrived on the verge of starvation. She was discovered near-death on the streets of Westminster by a clergyman named Samuel Worthington.

He ran a charity, St Barnabas' Refuge for the Destitute, on behalf of a wealthy benefactor named William

Lennox. Both took a shine to the resilient young Cornish woman. Worthington initially put a roof over her head and taught her to read and write; Lennox gave her work in his Westminster townhouse as a maid and later chief housekeeper.

"How did you afford to purchase Rose's?" Abby asked, being well aware of a servant's paltry wages.

"Mr Lennox loaned me the monies. I repay him each month."

"And you learned the coffee trade?" Jacob asked.

"'Twas hardly taxing. I roast beans, grind beans and boil water. A child could do it."

"A child, or Pasqua Rosée?" he shot back.

She broke into peals of laughter. "Jim Quigley! The old rogue is full of such tall tales!"

"'Twas he who told us that you are the one with tall tales," Jacob persisted.

"Believe what you will. I care not."

When Abby excused herself, Jacob found himself alone with the alluring proprietor. "Would you like another chocolate, Jacob Standish?" she asked, her tone as smooth as the drink itself.

"I find I prefer coffee these days."

"Aha!" She clapped her hands with glee. "You've fallen under my spell!"

As Rose headed to the fireplace to retrieve a coffee pot, Abby returned and hissed in Jacob's ear, "I discovered old Zebulon Strangeway in the print room."

He could tell from her voice that there was more to come.

"He's dead," she said.

Chapter Twenty-One

Elixir

Zebulon Strangeway was indeed dead. The old man was lying in the centre of the clay floor in the printing room, roughly where the inquisitors judged Eustace Blount's body had originally lain. His head was resting on its right side, bedraggled white hair splayed out behind him. His eyes were closed. He might have been asleep, but for the wound in his back.

Jacob knelt beside the body. "It must be the same murderer."

Abby joined him, staring at the lifeless form. "But the wound is different," she pointed out.

Strangeway was wearing a muddied, long-sleeved, cream-coloured shirt; in its centre was a two-inch-long slit, and around that a wide red stain.

"Aye," said Jacob, checking the victim's neck and finding no bruising. "This was no strangulation."

"Nay, Jacob, I meant Strangeway's wound is in his back. Eustace's was in the chest."

The old man was so light that Jacob easily turned him over. As he did so, he saw an identical wound on the front.

He grimaced. "This was no dagger. 'Twas a sword, there can be no doubt."

Abby glanced about the room. "Then where is it? And where's his Harlequin doublet? He went nowhere without it, yet he's not wearing it now."

Jacob was inspecting Strangeway's muddied shirt sleeves so intently that he did not hear her. "Look," he said. "Is this the mark of a hand? And here on his other arm?"

Among the stains on the quack's linen sleeves, the shapes in mud of individual fingers were visible. Strangeway's hands, too, were covered in dirt.

Jacob scratched his chin. "There was a struggle," he said, scanning the clay floor, which was only lightly pitted and marked. "Yet there are no signs of it here."

"How did he become so filthy?" Abby wondered aloud.

This was their grimmest discovery in all their days as inquisitors, and it occurred to them both: this was now their work. The housemaid and the naval apprentice, discovering the body of a man they had encountered but briefly, his life now cruelly extinguished. London in 1666 was no stranger to the black hand of death, but this… It shook them.

Abby stroked Strangeway's cheek, then pulled back, alarmed by the chill of his skin.

"Nay! Nay!" came the hushed, pitiful wail. "None would believe him!"

Neither inquisitor had heard the door to the printing room open, nor noticed Rose standing behind them. The distraught woman threw herself down beside Strangeway and pulled him close to her chest, quietly sobbing. "He was harmless."

Abby put an arm around her. "I'd no idea you felt so fondly of him," she said.

Rose looked her in the eye. "He was a gentle man, toiling to stay alive. The Mortimers scrounge off their wealthy father; the MPs of The Gilded Bean connive and corrupt for their riches. Quigley, I might respect, if not for his incessant mendacity. Zebulon was the only decent man among them."

"There must have been enemies," said Jacob, standing over them.

Rose shook her head forlornly. "I know of none." As she laid Strangeway back down, she gasped. "I felt something beneath his sleeve."

Rolling up the old man's sleeve, a sheet of parchment was revealed, tied with string around his arm. Sliding it down and over Strangeway's limp hand, Rose held it out for all to see.

The Most Secret Ingredients of:
Zebulon Strangeway's Elixir of Enlightenment

Small beer – one half pint
Treacle – three spoons
Turpentine – one half spoon
Tansy – small measure dried and crushed
Alum powder – one half spoon
Mandrake root – one spoon grated
Watercress – small measure dried and crushed
Oats – small measure crushed

Mingle ingredients thoroughly

Jacob groaned. "It is but one of the fool's quack concoctions."

Abby took the parchment, read it one more time, and placed it in her satchel. "Why was he here? Did he use the press?" she asked Rose.

The proprietor rubbed her temples, eyes tight shut.

"If we're to uncover his murderer, you must help us," Abby urged.

Rose sighed and took Strangeway's hand. "No one uses the press at night, when Westminster falls deathly silent, since its workings might be heard from the street. It operates only during the day."

"I asked whether Strangeway used the press."

Rose shook her bowed head.

Jacob, who had been hunting for clues around the room, was now lying on his stomach, pushing a lamp under the printing press.

"Have you found something?" Abby asked.

Grunting as he stretched out his arm, Jacob retrieved a large old leather case. "Strangeway's bag," he said.

Inside were small bottles and vials, clusters of tatty handbills, each advertising some miracle cure or other, dried herbs, a desiccated frog... Eventually, Jacob simply upended the case and tipped out the contents.

The inquisitors and Rose gazed mournfully at the pitiful remnants of a dead man's life.

"Hold!" Jacob exclaimed. "The bag still feels heavy."

Placing it on the floor, he reached inside and felt around. "Ah!" he exclaimed, as he pulled out a rectangle of stiff leather. "False base!"

Beneath it, he discovered secreted piles of handbills and pamphlets with titles such as 'The King's Betrayal of his People', 'The Royal Yoke: How the King's Social Order & Safety Bill Strangles our Liberties', and 'Freedom's Distant Echo'.

Abby picked out a sheet at random and read it aloud.

A Ribald and Unrestrained Tribute to the Dishonourable Members of Pomposity, Clement Culpepper and Jasper Davenport.

He passes his days in the grand Gilded Bean,
Plotting plans for the rich,
And corruption obscene.
Such a wit,
Nay, a bore!
His whole life is a caper.
Such a pig, such a prig,
He is Clement Culpepper.

His partner in crime is an oaf of ill health,
With a penchant for wine,
And plenty of wealth.
Such a card,
Nay, a blackguard!
He will never be caught.
Hail the lout with the clout!
Hail Jasper Davenport!

Under the poem were printed the initials 'E.B.'

"Eustace Blount," said Abby.

Jacob took the parchment from her. "The wits pen and print this slander, then Strangeway, who tours the public houses with his quack potions, distributed it."

Without a word, Rose pushed herself to her feet and left the room.

"More morbid work for Jim Quigley," Jacob called after her.

Before they returned to the coffee house, the inquisitors checked the far end of the corridor, where the store cupboard and steps up to the redundant trap-door were. Nothing particularly stood out, although Jacob swore one or two of the objects there appeared to have been moved.

Chapter Twenty-Two

Jacob's Local

Abby and Jacob did not tarry at Rose's after they had left the secret corridor, but instead walked straight out of the door. Neither wit noticed their departure, and the proprietor watched them go.

"If Strangeway's wound was caused by a sword, we must check those on the wall of The Gilded Bean," Jacob said as they stood outside.

Abby looked up St Martin's Lane and pursed her lips. The usual glint had deserted her turquoise eyes, and she looked tired.

Jacob noticed it. "Come," he said, setting off eastward along The Strand. "We should eat first. We will gather our strength and revisit what we have learned. I confess the sight of poor Mr Strangeway has troubled me also."

"What will I cook?" she asked.

"Nought," he replied. "I shall buy us a hearty dinner at an establishment close to my heart. You are an inquisitor, Abby, not a cook."

The establishment Jacob had in mind was also close to his home on Strand Lane. The Inn of the Bishop of Chester stood on The Strand beside Somerset House, dwarfed by the magnificence of the vast pale-stone palace.

Barely had he set foot inside the door, when the innkeeper, a jovial fellow with a powerfully scented periwig and a limp, was upon him. "Mr Standish! Mr Jacob Standish!" he gushed, ushering the tall inquisitor inside with a bow and a scrape. "How marvellous to see you. It has been too long, sir. Where have you been?"

"Hither and thither, Mr Puddifoot. Hither and thither. I am lately personal inquisitor to Mr Samuel Pepys, who is Clerk of the Acts to the Navy Board."

Abby dutifully trailed in their wake.

"Why, Mr Standish, that does sound most impressive! However, pray, forgive my ignorance… What precisely are the duties of the Clerk of the Acts to the Navy Board?"

Having blithely quoted the phrase on countless occasions, Jacob realised he had no idea.

"Mr Pepys oversees the working of the King's royal dockyards," Abby butted in.

Puddifoot at last deigned to notice her. "Ah! Mistress…?"

"Harcourt."

"Mistress Harcourt!" The innkeeper bowed so low that his chin practically oiled the floor. "And are we…?" He glanced from Abby to Jacob and back.

"Courting?" she asked.

"Odd's fish!" Jacob exclaimed. "Nay, Mr Puddifoot! We are…" he struggled for the correct term, "*associates*. Mistress Harcourt is my fellow inquisitor."

The innkeeper squinted at her. "Is she indeed? I was unaware that women were permitted to serve as inquisitors." Pulling out a chair for Jacob to be seated, he muttered to himself, "Whatever it is that an inquisitor does."

The Inn of the Bishop of Chester was a grand affair, boasting stables to the rear and dark oak panelling of the finest quality, which was hung with paintings depicting Somerset House and its distinguished occupants through the ages. A commemorative plaque on one wall explained that the palace had been built in 1547 by Edward Seymour, Duke of Somerset, and that it had been the residence of Princess Elizabeth before she was crowned Queen.

The furniture was functional yet elegant, and, from their attire alone, it was clear that the patrons were accustomed to occupying the higher levels of London society.

"Is this your inn of choice?" Abby asked Jacob, unconsciously eyeing his tangled periwig.

"Aye," he replied. "Since dismissing the maid, I find I dine here often."

"Your late father's annuity?"

Jacob nodded somewhat sheepishly. "However I have a trade now, as inquisitor. Thus do I earn my keep, which fills me with pride." He noticed Abby's head drop. "What is the matter?" he asked.

There was sadness in her eyes when she looked up. "My father would have been proud," she said. "When I saw the old man, Strangeway, lying there… It reminded me of him. I…"

She was interrupted by a serving maid, bringing plates of roasted meats and autumn vegetables, served with bread and ale.

The sustenance quickly revived her spirits. "We shall honour Mr Strangeway's demise by bringing his murderer to justice," she told Jacob, draining her small ale. "He will not have died in vain."

While they dined, the inquisitors planned. Most urgent, they agreed, was a visit to The Gilded Bean, to search for the murder weapon among the swords displayed on its walls.

The lack of a direct route from Thackery's coffee house to the scene of the crime remained troublesome. If Culpepper or Davenport were likely suspects for the old man's murder, they required means as well as motive.

"What is their motive?" Jacob asked.

Rose almost choked on her food. "'He's a pig, he's a prig, he is Clement Culpepper'," she quoted from Blount's poem discovered in the base of Strangeway's case.

"Aye, yet we assume the MPs are aware of it."

"Somebody is passing them information."

"Well, it would not be the wits! Thus, the spy must be Rose."

"What if the Mortimers have been pointing the finger of suspicion at Eustace, or Zebulon, to divert from their own sedition? They may be in fear for their lives."

"They surely do not seem it."

Abby smiled knowingly. "Men of that ilk are all pomp and bluster," she said. "'Neath the surface they are frightened small boys."

Jacob looked unconvinced. "What of the Bill?" he asked.

"What of it?"

"It is hated by the wits and sponsored by Culpepper and Davenport. Is it reason enough to murder?"

Draining her goblet, Abby rose. "We shall have to find out. I suggest we return to The Gilded Bean."

Chapter Twenty-Three

Back to the Bean

When Abby entered Thomas Thackery's coffee house, the muted reception was a marked contrast to her previous visit. Word had obviously spread among the assembled gentry that the young woman had powerful connections, and they greeted her arrival with sulky sidelong glances. Besides money, power was the one currency they all understood and coveted.

The inquisitors immediately spotted Culpepper and Davenport seated as before, and Thomas Thackery at his counter. The MPs cracked ingratiating smiles - *the weasel and the toad*, Abby thought to herself - while the proprietor maintained his disdainful glower.

Indeed, most of the faces looked familiar, smoking their pipes, reading their newspapers and belching their opinions. It was as if these custodians of the kingdom, granted the honour of shaping its future, had nothing better to do with their time than to sup coffee and pontificate.

"Pray, join us once again, Mr Samuel Pepys's inquisitors," Culpepper called out, causing Davenport to dig him in the ribs. "How is Mr Pepys?" he asked as they took their seats. "I trust you passed on my good wishes?"

"And mine," his companion grunted.

"I did, good sirs," Jacob lied.

"He recalled you both," Abby added, causing both men to sit bolt upright. "He informed us that he holds you both in the highest esteem."

Jacob glanced askance at his fellow inquisitor, and wondered whether they should have ordered that fourth ale back at his local.

He need not have worried, for the effect of her statement was instantaneous; Culpepper and Davenport began preening themselves and puffed with renewed vigour upon their clay pipes.

"You are most welcome here," a beaming Culpepper told Abby, as if he owned the place.

Hoping to catch them off-guard, she asked, "Did you hear the news concerning Zebulon Strangeway?"

Both men were a study of innocence. "No harm has come of him, I do hope," Davenport replied with mock sincerity, causing both grown men to giggle.

"Actually, he's dead," Abby replied.

The giggling ceased. Davenport raised an unruly eyebrow. "Pray, how did he die?"

Jacob pointed. "I see, sir, that you have your sword at your side. When did you last use it?"

One of the MP's eyelids twitched. "Do you mock me, sir? I will not have it! The last man who dared to mock me…"

Hastily, Jacob cut in, "Nay, sir, I would not dream of it! We believe the old man was killed with a sword."

Culpepper sipped inscrutably from his coffee bowl. "The quack was murdered?"

The coffee-boy appeared at the table. Abby declined a bowl, but Jacob accepted his, and they watched in silence as the brew was poured.

Culpepper pointed out the portrait of the King hanging on the wall opposite. "If 'tis a sword that you seek, then I suggest you begin with that sword that was, of late, displayed there, 'neath the portrait of our noble and majestic King."

There was indeed a bare bracket on the wall, beneath the painting.

"When did you last see it there?" Jacob asked.

The MP chortled. "Do I resemble a sword monitor, Standish?"

Abby coughed politely. "You're aware that the wit, Eustace Blount, was also murdered?"

A look passed between the politicians. "Good riddance," snarled Davenport. "The knave was a menace to society, and a hack poet to boot."

"He was no supporter of your Public Order & Safety Bill," she said.

Davenport erupted, his voice trembling with indignation. "No supporter? No supporter, you say? Indeed he was not, you insolent wench! Eustace Blount and his like, in that wretched hovel, are a menace to men of power and righteousness such as ourselves, who strive - for the good of the people, mind, though they do not deserve us - to bring order to their heathen lives!"

"He penned vile and scandalous verse against us," Culpepper cut in, when his colleague paused for breath.

Davenport's eyes began to bulge. "Aye, that he did, sir. And now he is dead!" Clenching his fists, he snapped his pipe in half and cast the broken halves angrily to the floor. "Blount thrived on chaos and anarchy! He stirred up dissent wherever he could! Do we propose the draconian measures in the Public Order & Safety Bill for our own amusement?" Culpepper tapped him urgently on the arm, gibbering uselessly, but the stout man was not for stopping. "Nay, we do not, sir! We seek to restore balance, to curb the tide of sedition and licentiousness that threatens to engulf us…"

Culpepper tugged desperately on his colleague's coat. "Jasper! Jasper! Quell your ardour, pray!" Turning to

Abby with a sickly grin on his face, he told her, "He means not what he says. He is overwrought."

"I am not overwrought, Clement!" Davenport bellowed, tugging his coat free. "I am fervent in my beliefs."

Panicked, his colleague added, "Which is that the Bill brings order and safety to the public houses of this city. We must tread carefully when voicing our beliefs, Jasper, lest we turn public opinion against us. It concerns me that…"

Davenport grabbed his colleague's silken cravat and pulled it towards him, until they were nose to pock-marked nose. "When we present our Bill to the great and good of this city, before the King himself, who is divinely chosen, it will be unanimously lauded. And we shall be lauded for it, Clement.

"Every caution has been taken to excise any clauses that might cause… consternation. I saw to it myself. Now, be a fine fellow and call for a fresh pipe of tobacco, since mine appears to have broken."

Chapter Twenty-Four

An Uninvited Guest

The inquisitors discovered that The Gilded Bean closed unusually early for a coffee house, at seven o'clock (when most opened until nine). When they asked Thomas Thackery why, he told them, "My coffee house, my rules."

As the MPs filed out into the chilly, barely lit St Martin's Lane, many heading for the nearest inn or tavern, Culpepper and Davenport cast the inquisitors black looks.

"I fear we may have heard the last from them," said Jacob, pulling his coat around him. "They will not speak to us again."

"Good," replied Abby. "They've told us all we need."

"They have?"

"Aye, Jacob. They knew about Eustace's poetry. Do you remember, when we first visited Thackery's establishment, one of the MPs accusing Strangeway of distributing seditious material? They knew of that also. Now both men are dead."

She let that sink in.

The distant guffaws of the departing MPs drifted back towards them from The Strand, and a lone sedan chair passed Abby and Jacob, carried by two trotting men wearing purple-and-gold doublets. An old man with a bulbous nose, long white periwig and a ribboned hat glanced out of the window at them, waved and was gone.

"Who was that?" Jacob asked.

"One of the MPs from the coffee house?"

Jacob was still pondering two Members of Parliament in particular. "You believe Culpepper and Davenport to be the murderers? They are servants of the realm."

"Davenport concerns me. The man is truly unhinged."

"Why use another sword when he has his own?"

"'Tis the perfect double-bluff."

"And the trap-door that will not open?"

Abby sighed. "Let's go home, Jacob."

Something had been gnawing at Abby since they became embroiled in the coffee-house murders: Jacob's political allegiance. She was not comfortable with radicals of any persuasion. It troubled her.

"Do you favour the King's rule?" she asked in a hushed voice as they strolled towards Strand Lane.

Horse-drawn carriages clattered past, hot breath steaming from the animals' nostrils, and dogs scavenged in shadows.

"Aye, for sure," he replied. "I remember well the years of Cromwell's Commonwealth, though I was but a lad. They were dour times of puritanical rule and harsh punishment. I would not wish to return to them."

She waited for him to return her question. When he did not, she volunteered her opinion. "I hear tales of the King, that he is dissolute and cares only for pleasure. When first he returned from exile, he arrived with magnanimity and made promises of prosperous days ahead."

"You believe he has not fulfilled those promises?"

Abby glanced furtively about her, ensuring no one overheard her reply. "I believe he has not, Jacob. Rife are the tales of the ladies of the court and his lavish spending." She added *sotto voce*, "He cares only for himself."

"You would return to the days of the republic?" he asked, faintly incredulous.

"Perhaps not I. The wits surely would, and I would side with them over those ghastly MPs."

When they neared Jacob's townhouse, both stopped abruptly. The shutters were open in the downstairs parlour facing the street, and the orange glow of a fire flickered from inside.

"Did you leave a fire burning in the hearth?" Abby hissed.

"Nay!"

"Then who…?"

Jacob sidled up to the window and peered through, then urgently motioned for Abby to join him. Silhouetted against the blazing fireplace was the back of a tall armchair, in which they could make out a figure seated, wearing a wide-brimmed hat.

Abby grabbed Jacob's wrist and squeezed tightly. "Who…?"

He shook his head. "Leave this to me."

Followed on tiptoe by his fellow inquisitor, Jacob tried the front door, which he discovered to be unlocked. Glancing behind, he whispered, "'Twas locked when we departed."

Abby's heartbeat pulsed in her ears.

Inside, the parlour door was closed. Jacob grasped its handle.

"Be careful," she hissed. "Do you not want a weapon?"

He shook his head firmly and showed her his fist, as if to say, *This is all I require.*

Counting down on his fingers - *three, two, one* - he barged open the door.

The intruder, somehow, was prepared for him, standing in the middle of the room, tensed for a fight. When Jacob charged, he stepped aside. The on-rushing inquisitor lurched forward, fell, and slid along the wooden floor, crashing into the wooden table on which his mother's remaining porcelain vase was displayed. The ornament teetered, toppled, and smashed into so many tiny shards.

Swiftly for one his size, Jacob was up and ready for the counter-attack.

Which never came. The intruder whipped off his ribboned hat and white periwig, then tugged on his bulbous nose… which he removed to reveal a nose of quite regular proportions.

"Quigley!" Abby exclaimed, the tension of the past few minutes evaporating in an instant.

"*Quigley!*" Jacob roared. "You terrible…"

"Mr Standish! Mistress Harcourt!" Quigley cried joyfully. "I bring assistance for your investigation. It was cold outside, thus I took the liberty of letting myself in. I do hope you don't mind?"

When calm was more or less restored (Jacob still simmered lightly) and the three of them were seated before the fire, the old coney-catcher took from his leather pocket a sheet of paper that had been folded in on itself twice. He handed it to Abby (which only increased Jacob's indignation).

Unfolding it, she studied one side, flipped it over, and studied the other. "Is this a jest?" she asked Quigley, who chuckled.

"Ask me where I found it."

Abby scowled.

"It was in Clement Culpepper's cubby-hole at The Gilded Bean."

"You stole it?" Jacob exclaimed, open-mouthed, and suddenly all out of indignation.

Quigley regarded him askance. "I am a purveyor of necessities, Mr Standish."

"You are a thief, Quigley."

Affecting hurt, the coney-catcher snatched the paper from Abby's grasp, pocketed it, and rose to leave. "If my services are deemed too unseemly…"

"Pray, be seated, Mr Quigley," Abby urged him, eyeing her fellow inquisitor reproachfully. "We are much obliged for your assistance. Are we not, Jacob?"

Jacob harrumphed, and Quigley retook his seat anyway.

"The page is blank," Abby pointed out.

"Aye," Quigley replied, wagging a crooked finger in the air. "It makes you think, does it not? Why would anybody pass an esteemed Member of Parliament a blank sheet of paper?"

Holding the paper over a nearby candle flame, he wafted it slowly from side to side. Gradually, before the inquisitors' very eyes, letters and words began to appear from nowhere. "Secret ink!" he declared.

"What does the note say?" Jacob asked.

Quigley handed him the sheet, and Jacob read aloud, "Nought to report." He paused, mulling the words over. "Nought to report?"

"I believe I have the answer," said Abby, and she went on to outline her theory.

The secret note, she said, came from Rose's, which they all agreed housed a nest of republican sympathisers. "Remember Davenport chiding Culpepper about his agents feeding him 'nought but scraps'. This is one of those scraps," she suggested. "The informant could not know that we told the MPs about Strangeway's death. Surely, then, they should have mentioned it? How can there be nought to report when a man has died?"

Jacob studied the writing. "Rupert, Vincent or Rose herself? Whose hand is this?"

"It may be another patron of the coffee house," Abby pointed out.

"We have not seen any," said Jacob.

Abby nodded. "'Tis true. You do wonder how she makes a living."

"I'm intrigued," said Quigley. "What is the reason for the murders of Blount and my friend, Zebulon?"

The inquisitors eyed one another, each hoping the other would go first.

"I believe 'tis a case of parliamentarian against royalist, wit against MP," Jacob piped up. "The MPs are too powerful. They will get away with murder."

"They will not," Abby replied. "Not now that we inquisitors are on their tail."

Quigley began pacing the room. "Yet you have not explained *why*," he said. "This rivalry 'twixt parliamentarian and royalist has existed for decades. Tens of thousands have given their lives for the cause. Yet here… It makes no sense. What could be the reason – of such grave import – that men have been murdered?"

Jacob could see tell that Abby was impressed with the old man; she was nodding to his words and watching him intently. Rising from his chair, he took the floor. "The reason is the King's Public Order & Safety Bill. Culpepper and Davenport's reputation stands upon it. The wits pen satirical ripostes, which undermine it and court popular opinion. That is ample reason for murder."

Abby appeared lost in thought. "Aye, Jacob. Remember this afternoon, Davenport, in his rage, let slip that the purpose of the Bill is not public safety but censorship and subjugation…"

"And those clauses that may cause controversy were excised by him from early drafts of the Bill," Jacob added.

Quigley clicked his fingers. "Thus, if you were to come across one of those early drafts, and made it public knowledge, the Bill would be in tatters!"

"Culpepper and Davenport might plot murder in revenge, and so forewarned we might catch them in the act," Abby added.

Jacob's eyes lit up. "How might we come across these early drafts of the Bill?"

Quigley clutched his arm. "They will be in Davenport's office. Most likely in St Stephen's Chapel, which serves as the House of Commons."

Jacob grimaced. "We would never gain entry."

Quigley, beside him, cracked a smile.

Chapter Twenty-Five

A Daring Mission

A plan was made there and then, around Jacob's fireplace, to break into Jasper Davenport's office under cover of darkness. During the day, Quigley said, the place would be crawling with politicians and soldiers. At night, they would have only the odd guard to contend with.

Having previously "visited" – as he termed it, and he declined to elaborate – St Stephen's Chapel, Quigley claimed to know the best route in and out for avoiding detection. "We travel by river," he told the inquisitors, "and enter via Parliament Stairs. The watermen use them often for visitors; thus we may avoid suspicion."

Just as he said it, the neighbouring church bells chimed ten.

"How many visit Parliament at ten of the clock at night?" Jacob asked.

"If you are frightened, Mr Standish…?"

He was, frankly, but he did not let on - because he was also rather excited. Jacob's fingertips tingled, and he felt light in the head. Here he was, plotting, by the light of a fire, to break into the House of Commons to steal documents that could ruin the careers of a pair of corrupt MPs who were also implicated in murder.

He wished his father could see him now... Although, as a diehard royalist, Sir Miles Standish would most likely be apoplectic with rage and demand an end to his foolishness.

Am I doing the right thing? he wondered.

"I wish to accompany you," said Abby.

Quigley looked at her almost sympathetically. "This is men's work, my dear. It would not suit you."

At length, it was agreed that Abby would accompany Jacob and Quigley.

She would wait in the wherry at Parliament Stairs while they stole inside, ready to move the boat if necessary, should prying eyes appear.

"If we do not return within half an hour, you must assume that we are captured and make good your escape," Quigley told her.

She nodded, having no intention of doing so.

Abby was aware - indeed they all were - of the consequences should their daring mission fail. Breaking into Parliament was a capital offence. Were there even the remotest chance of helping to save the two men from such a fate, she would not hesitate to take it.

What would Mr Pepys think? Abby wondered. She was becoming used to referring to him in that way - no longer as 'Master Pepys', but as 'Mr Pepys', since he had relieved her of her household duties and appointed her his personal inquisitor. She had taken a step up society's ladder, and it felt good.

It occurred to Abby that their current investigation, unlike the others, had not been commissioned by Mr Pepys. Here they were, conspiring against upstanding and esteemed Members of Parliament. He would be furious, she realised... And yet, he would also relish her story. *Mr Pepys does love a tale of derring-do!* she thought to herself. He would probably wish he could have joined them... But for the inescapable connection of their assignment to the King himself.

Am I doing the right thing? she wondered.

Shaking herself from her introspection, Abby asked with all the confidence she could muster, "When do we depart?"

Replacing his remarkably lifelike fake nose, made from *papier mâché* and wax, Quigley donned his hat and periwig. "No time like the present!"

The old coney-catcher led the way down Strand Lane. A sudden gust of wind shook the trees adjacent to Somerset House's ornamental gardens, rustling their autumn leaves. Besides the odd distant cry of a reveller or howl of a hound, it was the only sound.

They carried a candle-lit lantern each, fetched from Jacob's house. Quigley held his straight out before him, while the inquisitors hid theirs as best they could beneath their overcoats.

On Quigley's instruction, Jacob had changed into one of his father's lacy, heavily embroidered outfits, complete with colourful ribbons and bows. Sir Miles had been a powerfully built man, and though the doublet fit Jacob snugly, it was wearable. "Fear not," Quigley assured him. "The more ostentatious your appearance, the less likely you'll be suspected of subterfuge."

He had also made the inquisitor swap his own trusty periwig with a more extravagant one of his father's, and added feathers to his hat. Far from making him feel more confident, it made Jacob feel bare-headed.

At the bottom of Strand Lane, the Thames stretched out before them. Lit only by a half-moon, the gently rippling water appeared black as night, cut by tapering stripes of silver dancing languidly on the surface. Across the river, Lambeth, a nighttime playground for the dissolute, was dotted with lights.

London's church bells began their chime of midnight. To their left, the Thames was alive with craft crossing between the city and Southwark; to their right, in Westminster – the direction they were heading – the river traffic was considerably lighter.

"We will be noticed!" Jacob hissed.

Quigley took him by the forearm. "Quell your nerves, Mr Standish," he told him. "We are travelling to my house in Chelsea. Our journey is but one among many others."

"You have a house in Chelsea?" Jacob asked.

Quigley raised his eyes to the heavens. "That is our tale if we are challenged."

Descending a set of wooden steps to the Thames, he plunged his hand below the waterline and felt about for a while before pulling up a section of thick rope. Tugging on it, a small wherry began gliding towards them from the direction of Arundel House. Both inquisitors knew better than to ask whether it was his.

Jacob demanded to row, since he was the strongest, and had piloted his father's personal cargo-carrying lighter as a youth. Quigley had him remove all traces of finery so that he would pass, under moonlight at least, as his waterman, assuring him that the chill he felt would soon vanish with his exertions. The coney-catcher and Abby sat side-by-side in the bow; it made her feel safe.

The inquisitor's technique proved rusty, and they spent a while going around in circles.

The Thames tide was heading out against them, and, even once Jacob got going, their progress felt frustratingly laboured. At a snail's pace, they passed the Savoy Hospital to their right, then the fortified Durham House with its high tower. Abby, aware of the illustrious one-time residents of the house - among them, Henry VIII's wives, Catherine of Aragon and Anne Boleyn, and the adventurer, Sir Walter Raleigh - was disappointed at how dour and neglected the place looked.

They hugged the river's north bank, relieved to see precious few lights in the windows of the grand stone properties lining the shore. London was slumbering, which suited their purpose.

They were silent, lost in thought. Jacob fancied that even Quigley seemed preoccupied. Other river-craft passed them, most piloted by Thames watermen, ferrying passengers home at the late hour. One called across - "'Tis a fine night, sir!" - causing both Abby and Jacob to stiffen.

To their consternation, Quigley ignored him, and they heard the waterman curse.

When the other wherry was a safe distance away, Jacob berated Quigley. "Why did you not greet him?"

"I am a Member of Parliament, Mr Standish. I do not acknowledge the riff-raff," came the reply.

Having negotiated the bend in the river, they approached the Privy Stairs, where elegant buildings jutted out over the water on thick wooden supports. Just inland, they knew, lay Whitehall Palace and the court of King Charles.

Abby whispered to Quigley, "Why do we not use these stairs? I grow tense in this wherry."

"They are used by the King's courtiers and visiting dignitaries," he told her. "They will be too heavily guarded."

Passing a cluster of empty wherries moored beside the long wooden jetty of Westminster Stairs, they reached a sprawling building Abby recognised from an illustration in one of Mr Pepys's books. Known as the Star Chamber, it had once been a court of judgement, notorious for its harsh sentencing - particularly in favour of the late King, Charles I. It was well known for trying cases of seditious libel, a little too close to home, and Abby was relieved to see it now sat abandoned.

After what felt like hours, but was nearer a half of one, Quigley directed Jacob towards a jetty at the foot of a stout set of wooden steps. "Parliament Stairs," he hissed.

The tide was near full, revealing little of the river's sloping mud-bank. To their right stretched a high crenellated wall, over which they could see the silhouetted towers and spires of Westminster Palace.

The Palace comprised several lauded establishments - among them, Westminster Hall, the Houses of Lords and Commons, and the Exchequer - noted for their celebrations and ceremonies. At this time of night, however, it was rarely used. The hoot of an owl came from a row of trees just behind the wall as the boat bumped lightly against Parliament Stairs.

While Jacob changed into his father's clothes, Quigley tied the wherry to the foot of the stairs. Satisfied that his knot would hold, the coney-catcher stepped nimbly out, followed awkwardly by Jacob.

Abby appeared very small and alone in the bow of the boat. If she was frightened, she did not let on.

"Godspeed," she called out in a whisper.

A solid wooden door was set into the crenellated wall, which stood twice the height of Jacob. The inquisitor scratched his cheek. *Surely we do not simply knock?* he thought to himself, just as Quigley rapped confidently on the thick oak.

Jacob froze, horror-struck, and Quigley anxiously signalled for him to remain calm.

Footsteps approached, then stopped, on the other side of the door. There was silence for a while, then a voice. "Who goes there?"

"We are Sir Richard Pembroke and Sir Francis Ashby!" Quigley announced in a voice so rich and perfectly enunciated that Jacob felt sure it must have come from elsewhere. "We are Members of Parliament charged with urgent business on behalf of the King himself!"

Even Jacob felt convinced.

Following another painful pause, a heavy bolt was pulled back, and the door swung open, creaking lustily on rusty iron hinges. Stepping through, Jacob and Quigley were confronted by a guard in a colourful tunic bearing the royal coat of arms. His pike was held out before him, and his expression was hostile.

The old coney-catcher worked fast. Pushing the pike casually to one side, he strode up to the guard and told him, "You will wish to see my papers." Before the burly young man had even had a chance to reply, Quigley pulled a cosh from his satchel and knocked him unconscious.

Frantically, Jacob looked around, expecting to see a horde of soldiers heading their way. No one came running.

Beside the crenellated wall they had just breeched was a line of trees, beneath which they sought shadow. Quigley extinguished both of their lanterns; they would work now by the light of the moon.

Towering above them, a hundred yards away across ornamental gardens, rose the palace buildings. These enormous ecclesiastical structures, with stained-glass windows taller even than Jacob's house, made the interlopers feel very small indeed.

Quigley pointed out the grandest building of them all. "St Stephen's Chapel."

Stooping at a trot, Jacob followed him under the cover of the row of trees until they were level with the chapel. To reach it, they had to cross the exposed ornamental gardens.

With a quick glance around, Quigley told Jacob, "Come!" and made a dash for it. The inquisitor's decision to follow was not even a conscious one. Something beyond that compelled him. He just ran.

The next thing Jacob knew, his back was against a centuries-old stone wall, beneath the largest window he had ever seen in his life. He was panting heavily, and Quigley, to his left, had just disappeared around a corner. Instinctively, he set off in pursuit.

He almost ran into the old coney-catcher, who had stopped before a door. The much shorter Quigley beckoned Jacob to lean down so that he could whisper directly into his ear. "Behind this door is the clerks' wing," he said. "Beyond, you will find a corridor with a long row of doors on one side. Look for the sign bearing Davenport's name."

Registering that Jacob had understood, he tried the handle.

The door did not budge.

While Jacob held his head in his hands, stifling a long, drawn-out moan, Quigley produced a leather pocket from beneath his coat. Inside were assorted thin metal tools, some with points, others resembling keys. Selecting one, he pushed it into the lock, wiggled it around, and heard a satisfying *clunk*.

By the time Jacob looked up, he was inside.

Quigley pressed a finger to his lips.

With the outer door still open, a thin shaft of moonlight illuminated the scene inside. They were in a long, straight corridor that stretched into gloom. To their left was a wall hung with portraits and tapestries; to their right, just as Quigley had predicted, was a row of doors.

Using a tinderbox to relight his lantern, the coney-catcher beckoned for Jacob to follow, and they began inspecting the signs on each door.

They had discounted only the first two - Sir Edward Harrington and Sir Timothy Browne - when the absolute silence was disturbed by a sudden, raucous hacking noise. Even the usually unflappable Quigley almost jumped out of his skin.

Jacob made to bolt, but felt a hand grip his wrist.

Quigley was standing quite still, looking nonplussed. "Hold!" he hissed.

When the noise came again, they recognised it.

Somebody - a man, evidently with breathing issues - five or six doors up the corridor was snoring. Loudly.

No one came stomping down the corridor in a rage at being woken, nor was any shout heard, ordering the racket to cease.

Gradually, as the snoring continued undisturbed, Jacob and Quigley relaxed.

Making their way stealthily up the corridor, they located the door through which the snores were emanating. Quigley held his lantern up to its sign.

Jasper Davenport, MP

"*I thought it sounded like him*," Jacob mouthed to his accomplice.

The door was unlocked.

Leaving his lantern in the corridor, Quigley poked his head into Davenport's office and, once satisfied, signalled for Jacob to follow him inside.

The MP lay slumped over a large desk strewn with books and paperwork, illuminated by moonlight through a tall, leaded window behind. In front of him were a half-eaten plate of food, a jug, and a silver goblet that had been knocked over, spilling a puddle of ruby-red liquid. Instantly, the words of Eustace Blount's poem came back to Jacob.

His partner in crime is an oaf of ill health,

With a penchant for wine,
And plenty of wealth.

Still the snoring continued.

Scanning the office, hardly daring to breathe lest he wake the drunkard, Jacob spotted a set of shelves piled with rolled papers tied together with ribbons. On the wall above, a portrait of Davenport holding a wax-sealed scroll glared down at him angrily. Even in paintings, it seemed, the MP was in a foul mood.

Jacob began sifting through the piles of papers. 'The Petition of Right 1627', 'Crown Lands Act 1623', 'Act of Uniformity 1662', 'City of London Militia Act 1662'… 'Public Order & Safety Bill 1666 (Draft)'.

Jacob read it again: 'Public Order & Safety Bill 1666 (Draft)', and his heart skipped a beat. Ripping off the black ribbon that held the papers together, he moved beneath the office window to better read the content.

Flicking feverishly through the pages, his darting eyes alighted upon one paragraph.

Prohibition of Seditious Materials
It shall be unlawful for any public house to distribute, display, or allow the dissemination of any printed or written materials that could be construed as seditious or defamatory against the Crown.

In the version of Bill the inquisitors had seen, the clause was titled 'Control of Printed Materials' - no mention of sedition or prohibition. And that phrase, 'seditious or defamatory against the Crown', had been completely expunged. Jacob had it: proof that the Public Order & Safety Bill was a cleverly veiled legal manoeuvre by the King to silence his critics.

As he turned to tell Quigley, he saw the old coney-catcher wrestling with a gold sovereign ring on Davenport's bloated finger.

"Nay!" he exclaimed too loudly.

"Wha…? Wha…?" blustered Davenport, trailing a strand of drool as he lifted his head from his desk. The first thing he saw when he opened his eyes was an old man with a bulbous nose, wearing a hat more extravagant than his, attempting to steal his ring.

"What the blazes? Guard!" he bellowed. "Guard!"

Chapter Twenty-Six

Revelation

Jacob and Quigley stood before Jasper Davenport's desk, the point of a sword pressed into each of their backs. Two guards, alerted by the MP's cries, had intercepted them just as they were attempting to leave the administrative block.

Marched back into Davenport's office, Jacob still clutched the draft Bill in his hand. The MP, having cleared the detritus from his desk, sat there, gloating.

"Who are you?" he demanded. "And what is your dastardly business here?"

Quigley spoke up. "We are Sir Richard Pembroke and Sir Francis Ashby, sir. We are Members of Parliament charged with urgent business on behalf of the King himself."

Davenport laced his fingers together. "And what business would that be, Sir Richard, which is of such great import that it is conducted in the middle of the night?

Has the King perhaps taken a shine to my sovereign ring and charged you with purloining it?"

"Nay, sir. If I may?"

"You may not!" the MP growled, adding in his most unctuous tone, "His gracious Majesty need only have asked, and I would have given my ring to him gladly. Indeed," he fanned out his fingers, displaying half a dozen gold rings, "he may have them all."

At once, something caught Davenport's eye, and he squinted at Jacob. "Do I know you, sir?"

Jacob shook his head vigorously. "Nay, sir. As my colleague informed you, I am Sir Francis Pembroke…"

"Ashby," Quigley corrected him, trying to disguise it as a cough.

"Sir Francis Ashby!" Jacob blurted out.

Davenport grinned slyly. "Pray, remove your periwig for me… *Sir Francis*."

Jacob had no choice. But as the wig slid off, Davenport's demeanour changed.

"Guards, leave us!" he commanded.

"But sir…" one protested.

Davenport stared at Jacob then Quigley. "On second thoughts, take that one with you and lock him up," he said, indicating the coney-catcher. "I shall deal with this one myself."

"Sir…" the guard began to protest once again.

"Do as I say!" Davenport thundered. "And guard both exits."

Jacob watched as his accomplice was led away, expecting to see him forlorn and broken. Instead, he swore the old man winked at him.

Davenport poured himself some wine. "So, Mr Jacob Standish, personal inquisitor of Mr Samuel Pepys, who is Clerk of the Acts to the Navy Board. Explain yourself."

All the exhilaration of the night's escapade had drained from Jacob, and the enormity of his capture was sinking in. Glancing down at his hand clutching the draft Bill, he saw that it was trembling and willed it still.

Davenport noticed it too. "I see you hold a draft of my Public Order & Safety Bill. 'Tis a curious thing to steal. What is your game, sir?"

At a complete loss, Jacob let it all spill out. "We are investigating the murders of Eustace Blount, wit, and the quack physician, Zebulon Strangeway. We believe, sir, that you are involved."

The MP roared with laughter, rocking back in his chair. "My, that is priceless, sir! That I - Jasper Davenport, Member of Parliament for South Yorkshire - would sully my hands with the murder of men so insignificant they could be found in the filth of the streets."

Jacob slapped the Bill in front of Davenport. "You do not fool me, sir. Your Bill is a blight on the people, a means by which the King may control them. Your reputation rests on it, and you would defend it with murder."

"You are against the King?" Davenport's tone was not accusatory, more intrigued.

Something in his voice compelled Jacob to reply honestly. "In this instance, sir."

The MP drummed his fingers on the desk, brooding. "Jacob Standish," he muttered to himself. "Son of Sir Miles Standish. I wonder…"

Moving to the door, Davenport looked up and down the corridor before returning to his seat. "What I am about to tell you, Mr Standish, I do so under the pain of death. Should you breathe a word of it to anyone, I will undoubtedly hang. And rest assured, if that day comes, I will save a noose for you."

Jasper Davenport revealed himself to be a republican agent plotting the downfall of the King, whom he considered unworthy of the throne.

Ripping up the draft Bill, he told Jacob, "The Public Order & Safety Bill must pass, since it is a diabolical infringement of the liberty of the people. They will rise up, as they did on behalf of Parliament once before. Then we will rid ourselves of this worthless monarch, who is fired more by indulgence and debauchery than by the welfare of his subjects."

Jacob could barely take in what he was hearing. His thoughts tumbled and his ears were ringing. "You did not murder Blount and Strangeway?" he asked.

"I would have preferred that they lived. The more agitators, the merrier."

"What of your colleague, Clement Culpepper?"

"If I told you he was no republican, would you believe me?" He laughed. "The man is a dullard. His agent, the wench Rose, is marvellously evasive."

"Then who murdered those men, sir?"

Davenport shrugged. "That is for you to determine, as a so-called inquisitor - who was most fortunate this night. On any other, he may well have lost his head."

Chapter Twenty-Seven

Return to Strand Lane

Davenport personally escorted Jacob out of Westminster Palace, taking a devious route that avoided alerting any guards. When they parted company, he made the universal sign of a fellow being hanged by the neck, wagged his finger, and turned to leave.

The tide was out, and the inquisitor found himself wading knee-deep through the sloppy mud like an over-dressed mudlark. Following the bank of the Thames, he made his way back towards Parliament Stairs and the wherry. *How long was I gone?* he wondered. *Will Abby be waiting?*

Inevitably, she was, just as Jacob instinctively knew she would be. The wherry had become beached as the tide receded, and Abby looked frantic with worry.

"Where've you been? Where's Quigley?" she hissed as Jacob approached.

"'Tis a long story," he replied, wondering whether he dare trust her with Davenport's dangerous secret.

"Well?" she pressed, as he reached the boat.

Beckoning her close, he whispered, "Davenport is a republican agent."

"And he told you so? Why?"

Hands gripping the gunwale, Jacob clenched his jaw thoughtfully. "I wondered the same. He mentioned my father…"

As he pushed the wherry back into the river, aided by the slickness of the bank, Jacob's feet became trapped in the mud, and he toppled head-first into the muck.

It took all his restraint not to cry out in indignation.

Progress was easier on the return to Strand Lane, with the tide in their favour. At this late hour, the river traffic was sparse. Jacob rowed them toward the middle of the wide Thames, where they could not be overheard, and told his fellow inquisitor everything.

When he came to the part about Quigley's arrest, Abby clutched her face in horror. "What will become of the poor man?" she asked, though she already knew the answer.

Jacob also revealed Rose's duplicitous role as Culpepper's spy.

"I suspected as much," she said, to Jacob's surprise. "There were many small clues. Her expensive attire, the books on her shelf - *Leviathan* and *Eikon Basilike* - the secret-ink note in Culpepper's cubby-hole, and his use of my phrase, 'Only the fool speculates'. The poor woman has but two customers; it was obvious she receives funds from another source."

"We must interrogate her."

"Aye, Jacob, we must." She grinned. "Only if you wash first."

Chapter Twenty-Eight

Breakthrough

The sun had risen by the time the inquisitors returned to Jacob's house, utterly exhausted.

When Abby woke, she heard the bells of St Clement Danes and St Mary-le-Strand chime once, twice, thrice. It took a while for her sleep-fuddled mind to clear, so accustomed was she to waking at that hour of the morning, to crawl from her truckle bed in Seething Lane and begin work.

Then it dawned on her. "'Tis the afternoon!" she exclaimed, leaping from her cosy feather-filled bed to wake Jacob.

She found him blissfully unconscious, his mattress liberally stained with Thames mud.

"Wake up!" she exclaimed. "We've work to do. We must question Rose."

Groaning, he buried his head beneath his arms. "What day is it?"

"'Tis Sunday."

"Then her coffee shop will not be open," he mumbled. "She will be at home."

"I believe the coffee shop to be her home, Jacob. Re-member the blanket on her armchair and the chest by its side? Mark my words, she lives there."

A crowd was gathered outside the Church of St Mary-le-Strand, wrapped in their Sunday best, as Abby and Jacob hurried past, guiltily burying themselves in their coats. Neither had found the time to attend a church service since becoming Mr Pepys's inquisitors. They would have to make it up to the Lord – and their consciences – on another day.

The hackney stand was empty, and The Strand was closed for business. Jacob, awkward in gatherings – awk-ward in life, truth be told – often wished every day could be like Sunday. His fellow inquisitor, far more gregar-ious, had grown accustomed to greeting strangers out of necessity and did not share his view. Like Mr Pepys, she enjoyed a good sermon and could happily discourse with a stranger until the cows of Wales were driven to London.

"Rose knows more than she lets on," Abby said to Jacob as he hammered on the door to her coffee house. "We must break her resolve today."

"How will we do that?"

Before she could respond, a key turned in the lock, and she shot Jacob a smug glance.

Rose appeared in the doorway, as immaculately dressed as ever. "Were you speaking of me, perchance?" she asked.

Jacob chortled awkwardly. "Nay, good lady! We were speaking of…" He looked to Abby for help.

"Aye, we were speaking of you," she said. "May we enter?"

"'Tis a Sunday," she said, adding, "By the by, how did you know I live here?"

"We are inquisitors, Mistress Trewin," Jacob said grandly. "'Tis our business to know such matters."

As they followed her down the stairs, Abby playfully kicked Jacob on the behind.

With no windows, time seemed to stand still inside Rose's Coffee House, the patrons living in a perpetual dusk. Yet the proprietor appeared unaffected by the acrid air and constant gloom. "I haven't lit a fire," she said. "I shall, now that I have guests."

As she knelt by the fireplace, she asked, "To what do I owe this pleasure?"

"You spy for Clement Culpepper," Abby said bluntly. "I'm sure the Mortimers would be interested to know."

Rose's attention remained fixed on her coals. "I see," she said. "So that is where we stand. Are you blackmailing me, Abigail Harcourt?"

"I'd never do such a thing. We seek only information."

"If you know I spy for Culpepper, you must also know that I feed him fripperies and falsehoods."

Jacob spoke up. "The same fripperies and falsehoods that led to the arrests and executions of John Fryer and Henry Corbet?"

"Those men were careless. Their sorry end was of their own making."

"Rose," Abby said, prompting the proprietor to meet her gaze. "Who murdered Eustace Blount and Zebulon Strangeway?"

Without looking away, Rose replied coolly, "How would I know?"

Abby shifted her approach. "What drives you? Is it the fate of your family? Of your brothers, Gabriel and Peregrine?"

Turning her attention back to the fire, Rose struck flint against steel, sparking the tinder to life. "If you're trying to catch me out, you will have to do better than that, Abigail. My brother's name was Gideon, not Gabriel. As well you know."

As the tinder flared, an orange glow briefly illuminated Rose, casting her in a devilish light with her red robe and black hair.

"My point remains," Abby persisted. "How many innocent men must die before you tell us the truth?"

Something in Abby's words seemed to strike a chord. Rose's hands dropped limply to her sides, and when she turned around, the inquisitors saw that her eyes had filled with tears.

Jacob tensed, cleared his throat, and turned to inspect the notices on the walls.

Abby knelt beside Rose at the fire. "Tell me what you know," she said.

Their eyes met, and for a moment it seemed Rose might speak. But then, the connection faltered. Rose looked down and shook her head.

Abby gently took her hand. "Is it Zebulon you mourn? You were fond of the old man."

Rose shrugged her off, adding more kindling to the fire.

It can't be Eustace she mourns, thought Abby. *Then who?* "Are there other victims we're unaware of?"

"Nay," Rose replied, barely audibly. After a long pause, during which Abby willed her to continue, Rose added, "But there will be."

A chill crept through Abby. "Tell me," she urged.

With sudden violence, Rose pushed her away, sending the inquisitor sprawling backward. "I cannot!"

In an instant, Abby was back in her face. "You can! *You must.* Who are these men who will die? Whose blood will be on your hands?"

Rose clutched her head in her hands and wept. "You don't understand! Our bond is forged!"

'Our bond is forged'? thought Abby. *What does she mean? If she's protecting someone, then how do I get around this?* "If you can't tell me directly then…" She wracked her brain, searching for a way to unburden this woman. "Give me but a clue."

A pause in Rose's shudders gave Abby a glimmer of hope and she clasped the other woman's shoulder. "The betrayal of the miscreant would be mine to bear, not yours."

Face downcast, Rose remained silent.

"It would absolve you of liability," Abby pressed. "*Think of those innocent men.*"

Rose looked up, studying Abby's bright, turquoise eyes, flicking her gaze between the two dark pupils, seeking any resolve to cling to. Biting her lower lip, she barely whispered, "You missed something in the printing room."

Chapter Twenty-Nine

Discovery

Abby and Jacob stood back-to-back in the printing room, scanning the walls and floor for a clue they had missed. A clue that Jacob, having been quickly appraised of the situation by Abby, hoped would be the key to solving the coffee-house murders. *But what could it be?*

The huge printing press sat dormant, though the lingering scent of ink suggested recent use. The printed materials scattered across the clay walls appeared untouched—none added, none removed. No new words had been scratched into the walls.

"I confess, I am at a loss," Jacob admitted, scratching his scalp through his favourite periwig.

"It's here, Jacob. Somewhere," Abby urged. "Your eyes are more open than mine. They see things I don't. Look carefully. What do you see?"

He shrugged. "I see nought but a room."

A drip of water fell from above, striking his cheek and zigzagging down his long face. Both inquisitors looked up.

"The air grille!" they exclaimed in unison.

No matter how many times he jumped, even Jacob could not reach the wooden grille in the ceiling.

"Let me sit on your shoulders," Abby suggested.

Once she did, she managed to lift the grille, which was hinged on one side, and poked her head through. "Pass me the lamp," she said.

Jacob handed it up, nearly toppling them both in the process. "What do you see?" he asked.

With her head inside the hatch, Abby's voice echoed lightly as she shone the lantern around. "It appears to be an old priest hole, Jacob, nothing more. Probably part of the old manor…" She fell silent.

"What is it?"

"I see a tunnel! Somebody has broken through one of the walls!"

"I knew it! And I wager it leads to The Gilded Bean."

Abby shifted on his broad shoulders, gaining her bearings.

"Well?"

"Nay, Jacob. The Gilded Bean lies directly north of here; by my reckoning, this tunnel heads in the opposite direction."

"It cannot be. Can you climb inside?"

She tried repeatedly, but could not muster the strength to pull herself up. "I'm not tall enough. This hatch is so far from the floor, 'tis a wonder anybody reached it."

Jacob cursed. "I thought we had it."

"Aye, I too. Come, put me down."

"What we need," Jacob said, kneeling to let Abby slide off his back, "is a... Hold!" he suddenly exclaimed. "Why did I not think of it?"

"Think of what, Jacob?" She asked, wiping dirt from her hands.

But he was already out of the door. Moments later, he returned, carrying a wooden ladder.

Abby clasped her hands together. "The ladder from the storeroom at the end of the corridor!"

"Aye, why did we not see it before? If there are already steps leading up to the trapdoor, what would be the use of a ladder?"

"To gain access to that hatch!"

She hugged him, and he beamed like a child receiving a gift.

But the ladder did not reach the hatch.

It did not reach it by a distance.

"Was there a taller ladder?" Abby asked, a note of desperation in her voice.

Jacob shook his head miserably.

"We should at least investigate."

With reluctance, he followed Abby back into the corridor, and they made their way to the storeroom. Jacob glanced up at the nearby trapdoor, mounted the steps, and gave it an irritated shove.

Abby, meanwhile, was studying the large barrel in the cupboard. "Just as the ladder was out of place," she mused aloud, "I wonder... what use is a barrel here?"

The rim of the barrel precisely fitted the wide circular indentation Jacob had previously noticed, but glossed over as inconsequential. "When I saw the ladder and the barrel, that is all they were: but a ladder and a barrel," he said, clearly irked. "I saw them not as a means to a crime. It troubles me that my inquisitor skills are so solely lacking."

"Jacob, I missed it too; don't punish yourself. We'll solve this case."

Using the ladder as an unwieldy tool, Jacob discovered he could push open the ventilator grille from the floor. Then, after setting the ladder on the barrel – which was sturdy enough to hold firm – the top rungs reached perfectly through the grille.

With Abby steadying the barrel, Jacob began to climb. But no matter how hard he tried, he could not squeeze through the hatch – he was simply too broad. Frustrated, he still managed to make a mental note of their suspects' sizes and who might physically fit through the gap. Unfortunately, the only one he could safely rule out was MP, Davenport, whom he had already eliminated as a suspect.

"I shall have to go," Abby called up to him.

He stared down at her, his brow furrowed. "I cannot allow it," he said. "'Tis far too dangerous. We know not what fate awaits you in there."

Chapter Thirty

An Inquisitor's Lot

The tunnel stretching ahead of Abby was about three feet square, dug out from the London clay and propped up every few feet or so with wooden struts and beams.

The flame of her oil lamp barely cut through the pitch blackness; she was shivering - through cold or anticipation, she could not decide - and the space was eerily quiet. *What am I doing here?* she thought to herself. *Only a month ago I was laundering Mr Pepys's underwear.*

Although she was small enough to negotiate the space with relative ease, she still felt hemmed-in. The clay up there was not compacted and dry, as it was in the coffee house; it was damp and sticky, and within a few yards her hands were already covered in the stuff.

How long ago was this tunnel excavated? she wondered. It could only have been worked by one man at a time, she realised, given its narrow width, or by men taking turns in the lead. *One man? Two men? More?* she wondered. *And how did they remove the spoil?*

Just up ahead, the light from her oil lamp indicated a hole in the side wall. Intrigued, she picked up her pace as best she could, and discovered an alcove. Shining her lamp inside, she let out a small shriek.

There, wrapped in a Harlequin-style doublet, was a ceremonial sword with an ornately engraved handle.

Abby's mind raced. *The doublet*, she thought, *is Strangeway's, and the sword is the weapon that dispatched him. Was he aware of this tunnel?* She remembered the quack's fingernails being ingrained with dirt. *Might he even have helped to dig it?*

One thing was for certain: whoever killed him knew of the tunnel's existence.

As she continued onwards, she grew hotter in the stale air. Her dress kept snagging on her knees as she moved, and she hitched it up to her thighs.

Before setting off, Abby had dropped to her hands and knees in the printing room, much to Jacob's puzzlement. Stretching a hand out in front of her, she estimated her reach to be about a yard. Shuffling her knees forward to meet her outstretched hand, she repeated the process. It was how she planned to measure her distance in the tunnel - each stretched-hand length equating to one yard.

When she had travelled an estimated 30 yards, Abby paused to gather her breath and steady her nerves. The toil – and the extraordinary amount of time – it would have required to construct such a tunnel seemed almost beyond belief. *Whoever dug this*, she realised, *must have had an iron will, and a very good reason for doing so.*

"How are you?" came Jacob's call, echoing along the tunnel from the printing room. He had advised against this, strongly advised, and she was beginning to wish she had listened.

"I'm well!" she called back, hoping it sounded convincing.

As her reply drifted away, a sound caught her ears. It was faint, but it was unmistakably… *Aye*, she thought, *'tis running water.*

Ahead, Abby found another opening in the tunnel wall. In this one, however, was a short, sloping tunnel containing a mud-stained, wooden chute. Shining her light inside, she saw a stream flowing past the bottom of the chute.

The old River Tyburn! she realised, *which began in Hampstead and flowed into the Thames at Westminster!* She recalled reading that Tyburn water had once been routed through pipes to serve the residents of Cheapside. Later, it had been covered over, flowing through disused conduits.

Whoever built this tunnel found the Tyburn… and used it to wash the excavated clay into the Thames. How ingenious! she couldn't help but think.

As she peered down into the water, something shimmered in the clay wall near the bottom of the chute. Stretching, her fingers could almost reach it – but not quite.

With no choice but to edge into the sloping tunnel, Abby clung desperately to the slippery surface of the chute with one hand, willing the fingers of her other hand to make contact with the mystery object.

Suddenly, she felt herself begin to slide down the chute and let out a yelp. In desperation, she grabbed for the object and threw herself backwards, clawing at the clay wall for traction.

Lying on her back in the tunnel, her heart pounding, her hands and arms covered in grime, she took a moment to calm herself. Finally, she sat up and opened her palm, staring at the shimmering object she had just barely managed to pluck from its resting place in the clay.

As she did so, she shrieked and dropped it, as if it were red hot.

It was a small, white bone with a silver ring on it, engraved with a Turk's head.

Steeling herself, Abby retrieved it and slid the ring off, casting the bone into the Tyburn with disgust. Inside the silver band, she noticed initials etched into the metal: P.R.

She knew instantly whose ring it was, and now she knew his fate.

There would be hell to pay when she returned to Rose's Coffee House.

The journey stretched on, always dead straight, never deviating, for hundreds of yards. Abby began to fear her gruesome ordeal might never end. She was exhausted, and the musty air had grown increasingly stifling.

At several points, she noticed the tunnel walls had been widened, offering her the chance to turn around and crawl back to the printing room. She ached to do so - sincerely ached. But she knew she could not. She was an inquisitor now, and this was what she did.

Chapter Thirty-One

The Scroll

"Odd's fish, Abigail!" Jacob exclaimed as her filthy face and sunken eyes appeared at the hatch above the printing room. "You were gone so long, I feared you might never return. Thank the stars you are safe."

"Help me down," she gasped.

Abby sat with her back propped against the printing press, trying to recover her senses and stamina. Nearly every inch of her was caked in earthy-brown clay; she felt bedraggled and utterly spent.

Jacob inspected the sword she had handed down to him. It was the sword missing from beneath the portrait of the King at The Gilded Bean, which Culpepper had pointed out. It was, indeed, the murder weapon. But how had it found its way to the tunnel – and who had used it on poor Zebulon Strangeway?

"What else did you discover?" Jacob asked.

When Abby told him she estimated the tunnel to be some 400 yards long, his mouth fell open. "How long would it take to excavate such a distance?" he asked.

"Years, Jacob. Five, six, maybe seven? Whoever dug that tunnel is a desperate and determined man."

"What was at its end?"

"A makeshift wooden door, padlocked. There were tools scattered about, and the clay appeared freshly dug. I fancy 'twas only recently finished."

"You could not open it?"

She shook her head.

"Where do you think it leads?"

"The tunnel ran straight, due south from here. Where might that be? You know this area better than I." Suddenly she started, and began hunting in her satchel. "We must find Rose!" she exclaimed.

Jacob slid the sword into his belt, reasoning that it looked dignified there. "For what reason?"

Abby handed him the ring she had found embedded in the clay beside the Tyburn. "'Tis Pasqua Rosée's. The rumours were true. He was murdered, and his mortal remains later deposited in the Tyburn."

Jacob looked confused. "Why then do we seek Rose?"

"I believe she murdered him."

The coffee house was empty, and the fireplace was dark. The blanket was missing from the proprietor's armchair; the chest beside it was open, and empty, a discarded robe beside it.

"Fie," Abby cursed. "She's absconded. I fear we've seen the last of her."

"She may return to Cornwall?" Jacob suggested.

Abby laughed bitterly. "If she ever lived there, Jacob. I would trust not a word she spoke, now we know the true darkness of her heart."

"Yet she gave you the clue that led us to the tunnel."

Abby looked down at the empty chest. "Aye, something disturbed her conscience. The deaths of innocent men. She knows who dug that tunnel."

"She had ties to Culpepper?" Jacob handed Abby the water jug on Rose's worktable. "You should wash and change into her robe. It will improve your vitality."

"You sound like the quack," she replied with a tired smile.

"Which reminds me!" He reached into the single occupied cubby-hole on the wall behind them and picked out a rolled sheet of parchment. "I noticed it earlier, while I was browsing. 'Twas in Strangeway's cubby-hole."

Abby unravelled the scroll and read it.

To whomever discovered the formula for my Elixir of Enlightenment
Did you mingle well the ingredients?

"'Tis a clue, Jacob!"

"How do you know?"

"Strangeway's Elixir of Enlightenment struck me as odd."

"For what reason?"

"It included no woodlice, which are his favourite ingredient."

Abby reached into her satchel, rummaging among the papers until she found the list of secret ingredients they had discovered tied to the quack's lifeless arm. Scanning it, she spoke distractedly. "I was certain it contained a code, but couldn't find it. This scroll, I believe, is the key." Her eyes flitted between the documents, until suddenly she clenched her fist. "I have it, Jacob! We must make haste to The Gilded Bean."

"But 'tis Sunday night. It will be closed."

"Then you'll have to break down the door."

Chapter Thirty-Two

The Opened Barrel

It was dark when the inquisitors emerged onto The Strand, just as London's bells chimed the eleventh hour. Abby was relieved to find no one about; she had managed a perfunctory wash and changed into Rose's discarded robe, though she suspected she still looked a sight.

As they raced up St Martin's Lane, a large brown rat ran out in front of Jacob. Startled, he sidestepped wildly and ran into a wall.

"Hurry!" Abby urged.

The windows were shuttered at The Gilded Bean. When Jacob tried the door, as expected, it was locked.

"Break it down," Abby told him.

He stared at her aghast. "I will not."

She kicked at it herself, the flat of her shoe connecting with the heavy wood and jolting her backwards. The sound echoed up the street, and Jacob looked around nervously. "We cannot break in," he hissed. "'Tis illegal."

"Jacob, if I'm right, what's happening inside that coffee house is far more serious. Men's lives are in danger. Important men."

Jacob thumped on the studded oak door. "But 'tis solid," he said. "It will not be forced."

Sidling up to the nearest leaded window, Abby glanced up and down St Martin's Lane. Seeing no one, she drove her elbow through the glass. "Then we must find an alternative means of entry."

Jacob pulled his periwig down over his eyes. "You will alert the night watchmen!"

The window bulged inward, held together by its soft-lead framework, though a few of the small diamond-shaped panes had fallen out. "Help me," she said, elbowing some more.

Several anxious minutes later, they had snapped enough of the lead and removed sufficient panes to create a sizeable hole. The shutter behind it was easily barged open.

Sliding over the windowsill, the inquisitors were inside.

Jacob dusted himself down. "If I had known that being an inquisitor involved illegal activity, I would never have agreed to it."

The Gilded Bean felt unnervingly peaceful without the chorus of pompous male voices clamouring for attention. King Charles II and his father eyed the inquisitors sternly from their portraits as they made their way to the back door.

Once through, Abby strode to the trap-door.

"You will not open it," he told her.

One tug confirmed that was correct.

Jacob immediately noticed something different about the space. "Where are all the barrels?" He asked. "The last time I was here, the pile was vast. Now, but a few remain. Where could they all have gone?"

"What was inside them?"

"Coffee beans, I assumed."

"We should never assume."

Rifling through Thackery's crates, Jacob found a hammer and chisel, then began hacking into one of the lids of the remaining barrels. Soon, he managed to lever off a section and plunged his hand inside. "Coffee beans," he said, holding up a handful of raw green beans for Abby to see.

She frowned. "Something doesn't add up. How many barrels are missing?"

"Thirty? Forty?"

"Has Thackery sold that much coffee in the past two days? And if he's moved his storage then why leave these barrels behind? Shift them, please, Jacob."

Rolling the first of the squat kilderkins aside on its edge, he set to the task. As he was shifting the third, he let out a cry and took a step backwards, knocking over the opened barrel behind him.

Rushing to his side, Abby saw that Jacob had uncovered a trap-door. "That other one's a fake," she said. "A decoy. The real one was here all along, hidden 'neath barrels."

Jacob sank to his knees and groaned. "My incompetence is unforgivable."

She placed a reassuring hand on his shoulder. "Nay, Jacob. I would have made the same mistake. Our quarry is cunning." Suddenly, something caught her eye. "Look!"

The contents of the opened barrel, now lying on its side, had spilled out across the floor. First came a scattering of coffee beans – then a dark-grey powder, sand-like in consistency, with a faint shimmer.

"Gunpowder," said Jacob.

Both inquisitors knew of the Gunpowder Treason Plot of 1605. The conspirators, history told them, had been foiled. *Is this the plot revisited?* they both wondered with mounting horror. Dozens of barrels of gunpowder missing; the tunnel, dug patiently and relentlessly by hand, over the course of several years; their location, at the very heart of Westminster…

"Think, Jacob, think," Abby urged, wringing her hands. "Given what we know of the tunnel, what is the likely target? Is the again the House of Lords?"

Jacob shook his head distractedly. "Nay. The tunnel runs due south. The House of Lords it is too far west."

"Then where?"

"I have it!" Jacob exclaimed, dashing through the back-door. He returned in an instant, pushing a handbill into Abby's hand. "Strangeway handed this to Thackery, who hid it under his counter when I saw them.

An Exalted Competition of The Arts
Under the Auspices of His Royal Majesty King Charles
II, and the Esteemed Sponsorship of Jasper Davenport and
Clement Culpepper, Members of Parliament, all learned
Men of Letters are hereby invited to participate in a grand
Competition of The Arts, celebrating the Virtues of poetic
and prosaic expression.

Subject of the Competition.
Rebirth, Resilience, and The Royal Vision.
Submissions may take the form of essays, posies, or dra-
matic pieces, contemplating the future of our Illustrious
Kingdom, the Resilience of its People and the Benevolence
of the King.

The Prize.
50 Guineas and a private audience with His Majesty.

The Grand Reveal.
Banqueting House, Whitehall.
At eleven of the clock on the morning of
Monday, Septemb. 24. 1666.

"'Tis this morning, Jacob!" gasped Abby. "And Mr Pepys will be there."

Chapter Thirty-Three

Subterfuge

T he inquisitors left The Gilded Bean the same way they had entered. Nobody saw them.

As they departed, Jacob shared his knowledge of Banqueting House, recalling how, at twelve years old, he had attended a naval ceremony there with his father. While the speeches droned on, he had gone exploring and discovered the undercroft beneath the building.

"'Tis where we will find the gunpowder," he told her.

Abby was about to set off towards King Street and Whitehall, when he stopped her. "We will never be permitted entry at this hour," he said. "There are guards at the gate to King Street."

"But the King's life is in danger!"

He shook his head. "They will not believe us."

"But we are…"

"We cannot prove we are Mr Pepys's inquisitors. They will arrest us, and then we are undone."

Abby looked down at her hands, which were still ingrained with dirt, just as the tunnel diggers' had been. "Where's Jim Quigley when we need him?" she muttered to herself.

Instinctively, the inquisitors looked around, expecting the old coney-catcher to appear suddenly and take charge. But the streets were silent, not a soul around.

Jacob slapped a fist into his palm. "I should don my disguise as a Member of Parliament," he said. "'Tis what Quigley would do, were he here."

"Nay, Jacob, your costume is at Strand Lane, and the hour grows late. The Grand Reveal takes place in a few hours."

"'Tis our only chance," he insisted. "Come!"

She hesitated. "Nay, Jacob, my time is more wisely spent at Rose's. Now that she's gone, I can investigate unhindered. There are still clues to be found."

"So be it," he said, and with a parting wave ran off towards The Strand, followed by Abby's silent prayer.

It felt like an age that he was gone, and she spent the time combing the coffee house for insight into Rose's true history. By the time Jacob appeared, waddling awkwardly in his tight-fitting attire, she was already waiting impatiently outside.

"Hurry!" she urged.

Setting off down King Street, Scotland Yard soon came into view on their left. Ahead, the wide street, designed for royal processions, was walled off with a guarded central gatehouse.

The inquisitors slowed. They had not planned for this moment, stricken by the horror of what they had uncovered.

I should have come alone, Jacob thought, too late. *Or at least found Abby a change of clothing*. Rose's gown, though elegant – the coffee-house proprietor would countenance nothing less – did little to disguise the fact that Abby wasn't well-groomed enough to pass as the companion of an upstanding Member of Parliament, which he hoped to portray.

Up ahead, two guards stationed at the gatehouse spotted them. There was no turning back.

Linking his arm through Abby's – which, with their mismatched heights, only made his gait more ungainly – he told her in a strained voice, "Make pretence you are my wife."

When they were still several yards from the guards, they overheard one whisper coarsely to the other, "What the blazes do we have here?"

Both guards were wearing the same colourful livery, adorned with King's crest, as the one Quigley had rendered unconscious at the palace. Thankfully, he was not one of them.

The short distance to the gatehouse took an eternity to cover, their every step scrutinised with suspicion. The guards extended their pikes, though half-heartedly, as if placated by the presence of a woman.

Jacob spoke first, hoping to establish authority. "I am Sir Francis Ashby," he declared, "Member of Parliament for Huntingdon. This is my wife, Lady Abigail."

Abby did her best to look down her nose.

"We are here," Jacob went on, "as guests of the King, to attend the Grand Reveal of his Exalted Competition of The Arts."

The guards exchanged bewildered looks. "Sir Francis, the Grand Reveal does not begin until eleven of the clock," their leader pointed out.

"Aye," Jacob replied confidently, as if arriving in the middle of the night was perfectly reasonable for someone so grand as he.

A church bell chimed twice in the distance, quickly followed by many others. An awkward silence fell over the group, while the inquisitors attempted to feign the aloofness of the idle rich.

The lead guard spoke up. "Sir, 'tis two of the clock in the…"

"I am aware of the hour!" Jacob snapped. "We arrived by overnight coach from Huntingdon and," he almost blurted out that they had nowhere to stay, which hardly befitted the landed gentry, "as the Ashbys of Huntingdonshire, assumed we would be granted immediate admittance."

He felt Abby squeeze his arm.

The lead guard renewed his grip on his pike. "Nay, Sir Francis, that will not be possible. The doors will open at eleven of the clock and no sooner. I can make exceptions for no one, not even for one so…" He paused, looking Jacob up and down with a pained expression, seeking the right words.

Abby noticed the other guard regarding her suspiciously and was grateful for the dark clouds scudding across the moon, casting her in shadow. "We should depart, Francis," she told Jacob in her most dignified tone. "And return at the appointed hour." Before he could reply, she swivelled on her heel. "Come!"

Resigned to defeat, Jacob blustered, "This is outrageous!" Shaking a fist at the guards, he set off after her.

Once they were safely out of sight, Jacob turned to Abby. "What shall we do now?"

She pulled him close. "'Tis my belief that the villain is already in place 'neath the Banqueting Hall, but he'll wait until the hall is full and the King is seated. Only then will he ignite the gunpowder. I suggest we return to Strand Lane and try to rest - we'll need all our strength when the hall opens."

Chapter Thirty-Four

A Choice

T he inquisitors scarcely slept.

Abby was up before dawn, frantically scrubbing herself clean, to more convincingly resemble Sir Francis Ashby's wife. The time of reckoning was approaching and the situation dire - as each chime of St Clement Danes and St Mary-le-Strand rung in a new hour, she winced.

Shortly after six o'clock, while she was worrying what to wear, Jacob knocked on her door. He entered carrying a crimson silk bodice and skirt over one arm and a pair of heeled leather mules in the other hand.

"These garments belonged to my sister, Anne," he told her. "I have not seen her since she joined the King's courtiers; I doubt she will miss them."

"They're beautiful," she said, inspecting the fine braiding on the skirt.

"You are of a similar stature. I trust they will fit," he said, his voice flat.

She was about to ask if he was well, when the door clunked shut.

They arrived at the gatehouse outside Banqueting House well before the tenth hour, relieved to find a change of guard posted. Although they had to establish their false identities once again, the replacements showed no signs of suspicion, and they were permitted to wait until the doors opened to the Grand Reveal.

Abby, who fitted perfectly into Anne Standish's lavish outfit, knew the guards' credulity rested solely on her outward appearance. It mattered not who she was, provided she looked like the wife of a Member of Parliament.

As other guests began to arrive early in sedan chairs and private horse-drawn coaches, the inquisitors realised they were the only ones to have arrived on foot.

Abby was aware they could not afford to make any mistakes. "We must play our parts well," she told Jacob *sotto voce*. "Too many lives depend on us, and time is short. Draw no attention to yourself."

Jacob nodded curtly. He had known that all along.

In the queue behind them was a couple who insisted upon introducing themselves. They were Lord and Lady Everleigh, of Ashcombe Manor in Rutland, and they were keen to be noticed. Both were extravagantly attired in colourful layers. He had dreadful beady eyes, and she –

laden down with pearls and precious stones – brayed like a donkey when amused.

"You say you are the Member of Parliament for Huntingdon?" Lady Everleigh asked Jacob, while her husband peered at him disconcertingly. "We have friends in those parts."

"Indeed I am, mistress," Jacob replied, doing his best to sound unconcerned by her mention of friends in his supposed constituency. "How marvellous for you."

"I assume you are familiar with Lord Fitzwilliam?" she went on. "How is he?"

Abby felt her jaw clench.

Jacob took an involuntary step back. "How is he?" he echoed.

Lord Everleigh moved in next to his wife. "Aye, sir. Old Diggers. The rascal."

"Old Diggers, sir?" said Jacob, thinking faster than ever before. "Well, sir. He is indeed a rascal."

Lady Everleigh clapped her hands and brayed, causing the couple behind to cover their ears and the guards to glance over. "I knew it, Ambrose!" she exclaimed. "This fine gentleman is acquainted with Digby!"

Ambrose, however, did not look convinced.

The church bells began chiming the eleventh hour, yet the queue showed no signs of moving. The inquisitors craned their necks, hoping to spot Mr Pepys among the latest arrivals, but he was nowhere to be seen.

Lord Everleigh squinted at Jacob, as if inspecting something distasteful on his plate. "Your garb is ill-fitting, sir; it does not become you."

Jacob's eyelid twitched.

"Your posture, sir - it hardly befits a Member of Parliament," Lord Everleigh continued, prodding the inquisitor in the chest. "Pray, sir, what precisely is your function?"

As Jacob reached instinctively for his periwig, Abby interjected. "My husband, Sir Francis, holds a significant role on the King's committee. He is overseeing the rebuilding of London, following the terrible fire."

His Lordship turned to her. "How intriguing, Lady…?"

Is he testing me? Abby wondered. "Ashby," she replied, smiling.

"Lady Ashby." Lord Everleigh tilted his head. "I have a hand in financing this great endeavour myself." He paused, returning his scrutiny to Jacob. "Yet I do not recall ever hearing mention of your husband's name."

Jacob opened and closed his mouth.

"My husband is obliged to keep his dealings discreet, Lord Everleigh," Abby replied, stepping beside her fellow inquisitor and taking his arm, which felt as stiff as a tree branch. "His primary concern, you see, is the misuse of the rebuilding funds. Rumour has it that jewels and fine garments have been bought with diverted monies." Abby stared pointedly at his Lordship's wife.

Clutching at her extravagant pearl necklace, Lady Everleigh coughed, glancing nervously at her husband.

Abby seized the moment. "My husband hunts the blackguards. Don't you, Francis? How many have been executed, would you say?"

Before Jacob could garble a response, Lord Everleigh took his wife by the arm. "Did I espy Sir Edward Devereaux here earlier?" he asked.

"I believe you did, Ambrose," she replied, dabbing her face with a lace handkerchief.

"Excellent. Marvellous," Lord Everleigh blustered. "Then we must make our introductions." Bowing to Jacob, he added, "Would you excuse us?"

And off the Everleighs bustled, not daring to look back.

A palace servant appeared within the gatehouse arch. "My Lords, Ladies and gentlemen, your presence is requested within Banqueting Hall for His Gracious Majesty, King Charles's Grand Reveal," he announced. "Pray, make your way inside."

"How did you know Lord Everleigh had appropriated funds for the rebuilding?" Jacob asked Abby.

"I didn't. I merely guessed. They looked the sort." She nudged him. "Why did you engage with them? We were meant to remain inconspicuous."

"'Twas not my fault. The rich have a habit of asking nonsensical questions."

"Did you spot Mr Pepys?"

"I did not."

The royal servant led the queue of dignitaries (plus the inquisitors) towards the monumental Holbein Gate. Banqueting House loomed to the left. Guards were stationed around the walls, and a group of musicians with trumpets and sackbuts played a fanfare to welcome the guests.

Abby bit her lip. "Were Mr Pepys here, our word would be taken in earnest."

"Aye. What should we do?"

"I will enter the banqueting hall with the other guests to await his arrival. You must make your way in secret to the undercroft. You know the way?"

"I do," he replied, praying his confidence was not misplaced.

Jacob's previous visit to the house had been some years ago, but the layout of the entrance hall seemed unaltered. To his right stood a vast pair of double doors, through which the sounds of scuttling servants and clinking silverware could be heard. That was the banqueting hall, where, years earlier, his father's tiresome naval ceremony had so bored him.

Back then, he had slipped out and taken the door straight ahead, which opened onto a long corridor. There had been doors off to the left, one of which, he discovered, led down a gloomy flight of stairs to the undercroft.

Jacob felt Abby's hand take his, and realised they were outside the grand entrance to the banqueting hall. "Time is now perilously short," she whispered. "Good luck."

Then she was gone.

Moving purposefully, but not so much as to arouse suspicion, Jacob made his way to the door at the end of the entrance hall and slipped through. As he did so, he almost bumped into a servant coming the other way, carrying a pile of linen.

"Are you lost, sir?" the servant asked.

Barging rudely past her, Jacob intoned gruffly, "I am Sir Francis Fairfax. Member of Parliament for Huntingdon."

It seemed to do the trick, as when he looked back, she was gone. Hands on knees, he exhaled deeply.

The corridor had a high ceiling and was lined with portraits and wall-mounted candelabra, since there were no windows. Just as he remembered, the doors on the left were still there – four of them, with another further down at the far end.

Which one to take? he wondered, knowing that a wrong choice might open onto a room filled with servants, any one of whom might raise the alarm. If that happened, he knew they were all as good as dead. If he were arrested, the house would surely be blown up; everyone inside, the King included, would perish.

His Majesty may arrive at any moment. Decide quickly, he told himself, and reached for the latch on the first door.

Chapter Thirty-Five

Crossed Swords

J acob closed the door quietly behind him. He found himself at the top of a steep wooden staircase, hemmed in by walls of crumbling plaster. Memories of the ill-lit space flooded back to him. More by luck than judgement, he had chosen correctly.

However, as the gravity of the situation struck him, he was overcome by a stark sense of loneliness. *What fate does destiny hold for me?* he wondered, knowing full well how fickle a mistress she could be.

He knew who was down there, in the undercroft, waiting among the barrels. The responsibility of foiling this despicable plan now rested on his shoulders.

It was a heavy weight to bear for one so young and inexperienced. The lives of King Charles - and of his beloved Mr Pepys - were in his hands. *The hands of Jacob Standish, failed purser's apprentice.*

In his head, he heard Abby's voice, urging him on. Dismissing the creeping self-doubt - a curse he bore - Jacob steeled himself and set off down the stairs.

At the bottom was a heavy oak door with black-painted ironwork and a lock. When he tried the handle, it would not open.

He dared not barge it, for fear the noise would alert his quarry. *Then what?* he thought to himself, adjusting his periwig. Realising it was his father's wig, part of his disguise, he wrenched it off and flung it to the floor in frustration.

Slumping onto the staircase behind, he sat with his chin in one hand, tapping the side of his head with the other. All the previous days of fearful jeopardy and intense investigation came down to this. Foiled by a locked door.

How long before Banqueting House was razed to the ground? He could almost picture the devastation, having witnessed first-hand the ravaging effects of London's great fire.

Jacob thought of Abby up there, and, he hoped by now, Mr Pepys. They were counting on him. He was an inquisitor now - that mealy-mouthed purser was consigned to history - charged with saving the life of the King himself.

"Think, Jacob!" he urged himself through gritted teeth.

An idea struck him in a blinding flash. *Jim Quigley had faced the same obstacle*, he recalled… *And he had picked the lock!*

The only tool on his person that remotely resembled the one Quigley had used was the pin of his belt buckle. Releasing it hurriedly, something clattered to the floor. It was the ornamental sword – the one that had done for poor Strangeway. He had added it to his disguise as a touch of authenticity.

As he stared at it, his mind drifted back to his training in the art of sword-fighting, during his apprenticeship at Woolwich docks. That had not gone well.

He gagged his rising panic and focused on the lock, waggling the pin of his buckle in all directions, roughly as he'd seen Quigley do. All he could do was hope it would eventually catch. He did not expect it to work. He had no idea what he was doing, and anyway…

Clunk.

Had Jacob been able to pat himself on the back, he would have done so. But time was short. Worryingly short.

He picked up the sword and pushed at the door. It creaked as it opened. As he stepped into the undercroft, he felt sure he heard movement in the shadows up ahead.

Jacob gazed up at the vaulted red-brick ceiling, then ahead at a shadowed walkway, dimly lit by a pair of candelabras some thirty yards away. Each held a dozen flickering candles. In the farthest wall, he could just make out a door.

Standing stock still, he gripped the sword and strained his ears for any sound. All he heard was the galloping beat of his own heart, so loud that he feared it would echo around the walls.

"Thackery!" he heard himself call out.

Water dripped, mice scuttled, and time stood still.

How long do we all have left? he wondered. "Thackery!"

Moving forward stealthily, Jacob was alert to any movement. Peering into each dark alcove in turn, he saw only chairs, tables and crates.

"Thackery!"

As he neared the far end of the undercroft, a figure stepped from the final alcove on his right, into the central walkway. It was Thomas Thackery, proprietor of The Gilded Bean.

He held a levelled pistol in one hand, and a sword at his side in the other. "I wondered who it might be," he said. "Your voice sounded familiar."

The accent sounded markedly different from Thackery's, yet there was no mistaking the man standing defiantly before Jacob. He had shaved off his unkempt beard and, though his clothing was muddied from the tunnel, his face glowed in the light of so many candles.

Those distinctive blue eyes.

Jacob blinked. "Your own voice, Thackery?"

"You fool," came the reply. "I am no Thomas Thackery. I am Guy Kelburne. Thackery was a role: the guileless London coffee house proprietor. I played it well, do you not think?"

"Guy Kelburne?"

"Son of Anne Kelburne of Yorkshire – who was sister to Guy Fawkes."

Jacob's sword-hand dropped, and he shook his troubled head.

"I see you know my uncle's name."

"All England knows the name of Guy Fawkes. It is reviled throughout the land. We celebrate his death each November the fifth and thank God his heathen plot was foiled."

Kelburne pulled back the hammer on his flintlock pistol. "You would do well not to speak ill of the dead. My uncle was a God-fearing and brave man who would have rid this kingdom of its pestilent king. Now I am here to finish his work, which is my own divine mission."

Jacob took a step forward, knowing the move was foolhardy – pistol versus sword. "Your mission is an abomination. You will not succeed."

Kelburne smiled. "Pray, tell me your name, since it eludes me. I will know it before I slay you."

Jacob had hoped he was more memorable. "I am Jacob Standish. I am the personal inquisitor…"

"Aye, that much I remember. Standish, you say? Of the Standish family of Greenwich? Are you perchance the son of Sir Miles Standish?"

"That I am."

Kelburne bowed, keenly eyeing his opponent all the while. "Then I am pleased to meet you, sir. Your father was a man of admirable principles. 'Tis a shame he no longer lives, to witness this ultimate blow I deal on behalf of our movement."

What on earth does he mean? thought Jacob. Our *movement?* "My father was a royalist. He would gladly have given his life for the King."

"Ha! You are even more gullible than you appear. Your father gave his life for a cause far greater than the aggrandisement of a charlatan ruler. He gave his life for the people."

Jacob had heard it too many times now: this slander, that his father was some sort of republican agent.

"Thus, I shall honour you, Jacob Standish," said Kelburne, placing his pistol on the floor. "We shall fight to the death like gentlemen, toe-to-toe, with swords. I pray that you are well-versed in the art, sir, since I most surely am."

Jacob clenched his jaw. The last time he had fought with a sword, he had sliced open the instructor's hat.

Without warning, Kelburne charged, his sword raised in both hands above his head. Instinctively, Jacob raised his own blade horizontally and closed his eyes.

Kelburne sliced down with savage speed; the two blades caught, and Jacob managed to trap his opponent's in his hilt.

Their faces drew close. "I see you are no match for me," sneered Kelburne.

Mustering his not inconsiderable strength, Jacob lunged, sending the slighter man tumbling to the floor. Kelburne looked up at him, taken aback.

"What say you now, Kelburne?" Jacob taunted him. As he did so, out of the corner of his eye, he caught sight of the stack of barrels in the alcove Kelburne had stepped from. He noticed also the opening high in the wall above, with a rope trailing from it. *The tunnel*, he realised.

Just then, his ears caught the faint sound of crackling. There, on the floor, he saw a small, bright flame, sparking and smoking, moving at a snail's pace along a dark length of snaking cord towards the piled gunpowder.

"You have already ignited the fuse!" Jacob exclaimed.

"The moment I heard you at the door, sir!"

As he leapt towards the fuse, determined to stamp out the flame, Kelburne pushed himself to his feet and charged again, sword raised. Once again, the inquisitor caught the blow and trapped the blade. This time, Kelburne was on his guard and would not be thrown.

"I will not be thwarted, Jacob Standish, even if I must pay with my life."

"How long do we have?" the inquisitor asked desperately.

Kelburne leered. "How long is a lit fuse?"

The two men pushed against one another, their crossed swords inching first one way, then the other.

"Before I kill you," Kelburne said, gritting his rotten teeth, "I would know who betrayed me."

Jacob forced a smile. "The coffee-house proprietor, Rose Trewin. A woman of moral fortitude and courage."

Kelburne laughed so hard that Jacob was able to gain some traction, forcing him back a few feet. But Kelburne squirmed like an eel, sending Jacob lurching forward, and came at him from behind.

The inquisitor managed to spin and swerve just in time, the scything blow skimming off his thick coat at his shoulder.

The two men's sword-tips met, and they began circling warily.

"I sensed she would betray me," said Kelburne. "She has no stomach for death."

With that, he forced Jacob's blade aside with his own and lunged, taking the inquisitor by surprise. Reeling backwards, Jacob's heel caught in a rut in the floor, and he fell, abandoning his grip on his weapon, which arced into a darkened corner.

Kelburne was upon him in an instant, a leather boot on his chest and a sword-tip at his throat.

Feeling the whetted point puncture his skin, Jacob closed his eyes.

"I said you would be no match for me, Standish," Kelburne gloated. "And now you must die."

Chapter Thirty-Six

Negotiation

"Pray hurry!"

Both men heard it - Abby's voice, from the other end of the undercroft.

When Jacob opened his eyes, no one was standing over him.

Pushing himself up, he saw Kelburne slip through the rear door.

"There he is!" a guard shouted.

"Seize the traitor!" cried another.

Half a dozen armed, uniformed men piled into the undercroft; Jacob saw one push Abby aside, sending her sprawling to the floor.

"That's not the traitor!" he heard her cry.

They are coming for me, he realised.

Scrambling to his feet, Jacob lurched into the alcove where the barrels were stacked. The fuse hissed and sparked, mere inches from the piled gunpowder barrels.

As a hand grabbed at his shoulder, he flung himself onto the flame.

"Unhand me!" Jacob protested as he was hauled to his feet. "I must extinguish…" Struggling, he managed to spot the fuse; the flame was already out. He had managed to smother it. "Oh praise the Lord," he gasped, slumping into his captors' arms. But with Kelburne still at large, he knew the danger was far from over.

The guards' captain, resplendent in a plumed hat and polished breastplate, confronted Jacob, his expression filled with contempt. "You are foiled, blackguard. Take him away!"

Abby clutched at the captain's arm, staring imploringly into steely face. "You have the wrong man!" she insisted. "That is my fellow inquisitor, not Thomas Thackery!"

He brushed her aside. "Tell that to the judge."

"Abby!" Jacob called out, drawing her attention. "Thackery made his escape that way," he said, arms held tight by his captors, nodding frantically towards the rear door.

"Bring him!" the captain ordered, heading for the main door.

"Hurry!" Jacob urged.

Not one of the royal guards paid her the slightest heed as she slipped through the rear door of the undercroft.

An unlit flight of steps rose before her, leading upwards. Then the door closed behind her, and she was enveloped in darkness.

Feeling her way blindly, fingertips brushing the walls on either side and toes tapping against each step, she made her way upward. As the rhythm of the steps became familiar, she picked up her pace until a thin shaft of light, filtering through a crack in the door at the top of the staircase, guided her the rest of the way.

She emerged into a vast, airy corridor, with light streaming in through high, arched windows. Sensing a commotion through a large oak door to her left, she quickly made for it.

Abby found herself in the banqueting hall.

Four enormous, triple-tier chandeliers hung from the ceiling, which was adorned with a magnificent panelled painting. Elegant classical columns lined the hall on either side, supporting an upper gallery. Regal tapestries hung from the walls, depicting banquets of the past and royalty down the ages.

The floor was filled with tables piled with elaborate displays of food, with a suckling pig in the centre of each one. Men of great standing and wealth sat around the tables, dressed in their most ostentatious finery, many accompanied by their wives.

It ought to have been a scene of celebration and gluttony - but it was not. No one was eating... Or rather,

Abby noticed, only one gentleman was conspicuously eating.

Everyone's attention was riveted on the same scene. Faces were frozen in shock, some cried out in indignation, while others buried their heads in their hands, mortified.

Following the collective gaze, Abby saw Thackery beside a gold throne beneath a velvet canopy bearing the royal coat of arms. He held another man tight in his grip, with a dagger pressed to his throat.

That other man was King.

"Guy Kelburne!" Abby called out, for she knew his real name. Somehow, her voice transcended the general thrum and echoed about the banqueting hall.

At once, all eyes were on her.

Kelburne twisted to view her approach, pulling the King with him. His polished blade caught sunlight through one of the windows, briefly dazzling the advancing inquisitor.

The two men were surrounded by royal guards, some with swords drawn, others with muskets and pistols trained on Kelburne. Abby knew they dared not risk a shot; the King's head was pressed tightly against Kelburne's. An inch out, and the King would die.

"Stay back!" Kelburne warned them. "Or your precious monarch dies."

"Do as he says!" Charles ordered. His tone sounded relaxed, almost withering. Abby assumed he was bluffing.

As she drew closer, she saw the King's crown lying on the floor, presumably the result of a scuffle... and there, behind the two men, previously obscured from her view, another man prone on the tiles. She recognised him immediately: it was Mr Pepys. To her great relief, she noticed his fingers moving, as if he were regaining consciousness.

"Hold there!" Kelburne ordered when she was some ten yards away. "I know you, do I not?"

Abby ignored him. "What do you hope to achieve? You cannot escape."

Kelburne glanced around at the poised guards. None would make a move while the point of his dagger rested at the King's throat, and he knew it. "I am the nephew of Guy Fawkes!" he declared.

The name drew gasps from all assembled.

Even King Charles himself looked momentarily taken aback, but quickly recovered his composure. "And you will follow him to the gallows," he said, "as surely as day follows night."

Kelburne drew his blade along the King's neck. "Your bloodline means nought to those who seek liberty, Charles Stuart. Your crown falls today, and with it your legacy. England shall be returned to its people."

Abby noticed Mr Pepys, directly behind and below Kelburne's eyeline, beginning to stir. As he lifted his head and registered the King's peril, a look of horror crossed his face. He was on the verge of crying out when his eyes met Abby's. Discreetly, she motioned for him to stay still.

"Why did you kill Eustace Blount?" she demanded of Kelburne, keeping his attention away from Pepys.

The guests murmured their outrage, although few could have known the wit.

Kelburne forced a wry laugh. "I remember you now - you're the companion of that fool from the undercroft. Why so interested in Blount? The poor fool had admirable political intentions, but he found my tunnel. He had to die."

"You strangled him?"

"What consequence is the manner of his death? However, if you must know, I strangled him then implicated the quack. It served my purpose."

Pepys began crawling the short distance toward the entangled King and Kelburne, his face a mask of pure fear.

Seeing him do so - desperately trying not to stare - Abby sought to keep the assailant's focus. "You murdered Strangeway also. Why?"

"The tunnel was completed, his work was done..." Abruptly, Kelburne fell silent and smiled. "Are you attempting to beguile me, little lady?" Once again, he glanced around at the guards. "I fear our time for talk is over! If I must die, then I shall take this tyrant King with me…"

"Hold!" Abby cried out, her voice choked with panic.

Pepys had managed to reach Kelburne's heels undetected, anxiously waiting for a signal from Abby.

"Look at me, Kelburne!" she urged, terrified that he might glance down and spot Pepys.

"The time for talk is over, I said!"

He meant it, and Abby knew it. She played her hand. "What say you to the name Ursula Winter?"

Kelburne physically jolted, such was the shock of hearing Ursula's name. His head dropped, his grip on Charles slackened, and the hand holding the dagger faltered.

"Now!" Abby screamed.

Clutching each of Kelburne's ankles, Pepys yanked backwards with all his might as the King instinctively threw himself to one side. Crying out, Kelburne toppled forward and crashed to the floor. Within moments, he was clasped firmly in the hands of the royal guard.

It was over.

Chapter Thirty-Seven

By Royal Invitation

Once the situation had been explained to the authorities, Jacob was released. Two extra places were set at Mr Pepys's table and the inquisitors were reunited, Abby seated between the two men. The pair began relating their exploits, but found themselves constantly interrupted.

Pepys's and Abby's heroics had become the toast of the banquet, leaving Jacob to sulk into his goblet. "I know how brave you were, Jacob," Abby told him, "and that's all that truly matters."

"Hardly," he muttered, casting an idle glance at the queue of glad-handers.

Their employer was especially full of himself - as well he might be, having just saved the King's life. "Did you see how I toppled the devil?" he asked eagerly, gulping down wine, as they politely indulged him in the umpteenth retelling.

Halfway through the story - Pepys was just reviving, having been knocked unconscious by Kelburne while discoursing with His Majesty - Abby excused herself.

There had been but one man who appeared entirely untroubled by the King's kidnapping, she suddenly remembered. He had gorged himself throughout the ordeal, and she was curious.

As she made her way past the tables of guests, she spotted the MPs, Clement Culpepper and Jasper Davenport. Culpepper rose and bowed obsequiously; Davenport merely glowered, disdain writ across his grease-stained face.

I know why you're so upset, she thought, smiling to herself.

Abby's quarry was seated at the next table along, wearing an outrageous hat-and-periwig combination… and he appeared to be surreptitiously bagging the King's silverware.

Said gentleman was out of his seat even before Abby reached him.

"Mistress Abigail Harcourt!" he declared, swiping off his hat and bowing lavishly. "'Tis an honour to be granted an audience with the King's saviour."

"Sir Richard Pembroke, I assume?" she replied, returning the bow. "The pleasure is all mine. Pray tell, what brings you here?"

"The food is most excellent," he replied, adding from the corner of his mouth, "*and gratis.*" Checking that his dining companions' attentions were diverted elsewhere, he furtively opened a sack secreted beneath the table, exposing a silver candlestick, several plates and dishes, a gentleman's silk handkerchief and a sleeping spaniel.

Taking his arm, Abby pulled him close and hissed in his ear, "How did you escape jail, Quigley?"

The old coney-catcher tapped his nose. "I knew the jailer, mistress, and we agreed a deal." He beamed. "I exchanged my freedom for a sow."

"Abigail! Abigail!" Pepys urgently beckoned her to return to their table. "I have so many questions for you!" When she was seated beside him, he added furtively, "Mr Standish has not been terribly forthcoming."

"What do you wish to know, sir?"

"Who on earth is Ursula Winter?"

Delving into her satchel, Abby produced an amateur-ishly handwritten playbill that she placed on the table. She had found it last night, she explained, secreted between the pages of a book at Rose's Coffee House, while Jacob changed into his disguise at Strand Lane.

The Crowning of a King
Or
England's Shameful Folly
By

Guy Kelburne

CAST

Queen Henrietta Maria … Ursula Winter
Thomas Thackery … Guy Kelburne
King Charles … Percival Winter
William Laud … Bertram Winter
Rose Trewin … Dorcas Winter

On it was scrawled a note that read: *If you have time for me, as I believe you do, seek me out in London. Guy.*

"You knew Thackery was, in truth, Guy Kelburne?" Jacob asked.

"Aye. And the coffee-house proprietor, Rose Trewin, was Dorcas Winter. Both were assumed names, taken from a play Kelburne himself had written."

A servant appeared, hovering nearby, ready to replenish their goblets.

Pepys downed his in one and held out the vessel for more. "*Who was Ursula*, Abigail? 'Twas the mention of her name that confounded Kelburne so, which allowed me to save the King's life."

"Sir, I believe I was also…" Jacob began.

"Hush, Jacob," Abby interjected, patting his hand. "Since Kelburne wrote the play and made Ursula his lead, I surmised they'd been lovers. I found her name in the King's personal testimony, *Eikon Basilike*, on Rose's shelf - she was executed for treason in 1627. The very mention of her name would, I hoped, strike to his heart. Praise the Lord, I was right."

"Ursula and Dorcas Winter?" Pepys mused, goblet poised before his lips. "The Winter brothers, Thomas and Robert, conspired with Guy Fawkes in the dreadful Gunpowder Treason Plot."

Abby folded the playbill. "Aye, sir, it seems certain both she and Kelburne share Plotters' blood. They acted in collusion. I believe Pasqua Rosée made the original purchase of her coffee house, and she or Kelburne murdered him for it.

"Jacob discovered a token from Rosée's original coffee house in an alcove within a secret corridor at Rose's, where his body was first hidden. When the wits moved in and discovered the corridor, it was transferred to Kelburne's tunnel, which was already in progress."

"Why two coffee houses?" Pepys asked. "When one would have sufficed?"

Abby shrugged. "I assume they wished to act separately, to conceal their dealings."

Pepys suddenly clapped his hands. "I have it! How exquisitely witty!" he exclaimed. "Winter/Trewin. 'Tis an anagram!"

Jacob, who had been lost in thought, grabbed Abby's hand and shook it. "I have it also! The sign outside Rose's Coffee House. It had been spliced and repaired, removing the 'é' from Rosée – thus, it spelled Rose!"

Abby smirked at seeing the men so pleased with themselves. "Aye, Jacob," she said. "'Tis why it read "COFEE HOSE'. The woman had no money. Only that which she earned later, spying for Culpepper. Her supposed benefactor, Lennox, was a figment of her imagination."

A servant appeared beside Pepys and whispered in his ear. When he left, Pepys stood, motioning for his inquisitors to do the same. "We have been summoned to an audience with His Majesty," he told them.

The three gathered before the throne. Although Abby and Jacob had both witnessed royal processions in London's streets before, never had they been so close to the King himself. When Abby noticed Jacob's hands were trembling, she realised she too felt overawed.

His Majesty wore a richly embroidered velvet doublet in dark blue, inlaid with precious gemstones. His wide collar and elaborate cuffs were made of lace, and he wore a deep-brown periwig topped off with a plumed hat. He had a prominent nose and an expressive face.

Much bowing dispensed with, Charles beckoned Abby forward, took her hand, and kissed it. He seemed taller than she had expected.

"My, what a handsome young lady you are," he said. "Such exquisite eyes."

The inquisitor's pale, freckled cheeks turned a vivid shade of red, and she began stumbling for her words. "I… Why, Your Majesty…"

The King silenced her. "What is your name, pray?"

"Abigail Harcourt," she heard herself reply.

"You must visit me at my court, Mistress Harcourt," he told her with a smile, then turning to her employer added, "See to it, will you, Pepys?"

With that, a hovering servant handed His Majesty a leather pouch, which he passed on to Pepys. "A token of my esteem," said Charles. "I am in your debt." He turned his gaze on Jacob. "You, sir."

"Jacob Standish, sir. Personal inquisitor to Mr Samuel Pepys, who is Clerk of the Acts to the Navy Board," the inquisitor blurted out.

The King laughed, flashing discoloured teeth. "I am well acquainted with Mr. Pepys and his work, as it is my Navy Board. By the by, are you kin to Sir Miles Standish?"

Jacob emitted a strangled sound, faintly resembling assent.

"One of my staunchest allies, and greatly missed," Charles went on. "And you are much like him, sir, since you did foil, I am told, a second Gunpowder Treason Plot here in Banqueting House, under our very noses?"

Dearly wishing he had not left his trusty periwig back at Strand Lane, Jacob could only nod, his mouth frozen into a rictus grin.

"You may step forward and kiss my hand, Mr Standish," the King told him. "I am in your debt, sir."

Despite his nerves, Jacob was able to complete the manoeuvre without making a fool of himself, and the audience was ended with a regal wave of the hand. When the three of them returned to their table, their fellow diners were silently seething with jealousy.

Taking his seat, Jacob nudged Abby. "The King would have you as his courtier," he said.

Looking him in the eyes, she replied in a whisper, "I can imagine nought worse."

Pepys, ever vigilant for gossip, overheard their exchange. "You cannot refuse him, Abigail. He is the King."

"And his reputation as a philanderer precedes him," she muttered in reply.

Pepys pulled her close. "Consorting with the King will only enhance your own reputation." When she looked unimpressed, he added, "Remember the coffee house on Fleet Street? The Rainbow, from which you were once barred? The proprietor, Mr Farr, would crave your patronage were you acquainted with His Majesty."

Abby grimaced. "I would not wish it, sir. I find I have had my fill of men's coffee houses. They may keep them."

Seeing their fellow diners now whispering among themselves and glancing in his direction, Pepys quickly changed the subject. The talk turned returned to the recent investigation.

"This quack, Strangeway, and Kelburne excavated the tunnel between them?" he asked Abby, savouring his Haut-Brion. "And when it was completed, Kelburne murdered the fellow?"

"Aye, sir," Abby replied, selecting a hunk of beef from a vast tray of roasted meats. "Kelburne, posing as Thackery, closed his coffee house early each night, for he and his republican ally, Strangeway, to dig their tunnel. Both men looked tired, and, though they scrubbed at the dirt, it was ingrained in their fingers. It was the first clue that I missed."

"Which clue?" Jacob asked.

"The bruise on Blount's neck appeared earthy brown. It was no bruise, Jacob; it was clay, from Kelburne's hands. Unfortunately, the body was disposed of before I could inspect it more closely."

Pepys shook his head in admiration. "And when did you first suspect the devil?"

"Strangeway was summoned to Rose's Coffee House to implicate him in the murder of the wit, Eustace Blount, who had stumbled upon the tunnel late one night. Blount appeared to have been stabbed with a dagger, which Strangeway carried.

"The old man told us he suspected who had done so. It was Kelburne, we now know, who wanted rid of him, presumably as the key witness to their treachery.

"I believe Blount's wound was caused not by a dagger, but by the chisel in the store cupboard. I noticed it when I searched for clues at Rose's Coffee House. What appeared to be rust on the chisel, I now suspect was dried blood.

"When Strangeway was found dead, if I was right about the dirt on Blount's neck, one of the two men with filth-ingrained hands was gone. Which left only Kelburne."

"That is mere supposition, Abigail," Pepys pointed out.

"Aye, sir. However, Strangeway confirmed it. Fearing that Kelburne had murder in mind, he secreted about his person a clue to his identity, disguised as a list of ingredients. The key to its solution, he hid elsewhere, thus avoiding arousing Kelburne's suspicions."

Abby showed Pepys the list, explaining that the initial letters of the ingredients spelled out 'STTTAMWO', which had made no sense to her. "Unfortunately, I paid no heed to Strangeway's instruction to 'Mingle ingredients thoroughly' - until Jacob found the clue in the scroll. Mingle the letters and it becomes 'T'WAS TOM T'. 'T'was Thomas Thackery'. 'Tis another anagram, sir."

"Thus the quack identified his murderer from beyond the grave!" exclaimed Pepys. "What an ingenious fellow."

Pepys stretched out his arms and sighed contentedly. "A most excellent investigation, even if it was not one of my own devising."

Throwing his arms in the air, Jacob exclaimed, "Mr Pepys, sir! Your pocket watch! Amidst all…"

Reaching inside his coat, Pepys pulled out a brass pocket watch. The inquisitors stared at it, agog. "This pocket watch?" Pepys asked.

"Sir, is that…?"

"Aye, Mr Standish, 'tis the timepiece in question. It was handed to me by a most agreeable gentleman. A Member of Parliament, no less." Pepys was too busy pontificating to notice the grin spreading across Abby's face. "He informed me that he found it on the floor of a coffee house and did notice my name engraved therein. His name was… Aye, 'twas Sir Richard Pembroke." Pepys gestured towards a table across the room. "Indeed, there is the fine fellow now."

Jacob gripped the edge of the table. "Quigley!" he thundered.

If you enjoyed this book, please consider leaving a review –
they are greatly appreciated and genuinely help.

"This series just gets better with every book" – *Rambling Mads*

Amazon link: mybook.to/pepys-series.

Where next?

A SAMUEL PEPYS MYSTERY
MYSTERY
ELLIS · BLACKWOOD
The King's Court Murders

The King's mistresses are being murdered one by one…

Ellis Blackwood

E llis Blackwood fell in love with the writings of Samuel Pepys, and the 17th-century England he so colourfully portrays, via the great man's published diaries. The Samuel Pepys Mysteries are the result of that literary love affair.

Ellis lives on the coast of Cornwall with his wife, two daughters and dog, Spike. A former journalist, he wrote features for many of the UK's most popular national newspapers and magazines. He recently gained an MA in Comedy Writing from Falmouth University.

The Samuel Pepys Mysteries
Book 0.5: Mr Pepys's Stolen Diaries
Book 1: The Brampton Witch Murders
Book 2: The Plague Doctor Murders
Book 3: The Coffee House Murders
Book 4: The King's Court Murders
Book 5: The Frost Fair Murders
Book 6: The Drury Lane Murders

I'm on Facebook and Instagram. Love to hear your thoughts, always happy to answer questions. Find all my links using this QR code:

Acknowledgements

I could not have published The Coffee House Murders without the sterling work of Tim Brown, whose covers are a joy to behold, and whose editorial guidance has been a godsend. Equally, my wife, Sinead, has worked tirelessly and generously in the background to allow me the time and space to write The Pepys Mysteries.

If you'd like to learn more about Samuel Pepys, the Restoration period and London's coffee houses, I recommend starting here:

- *All About Coffee* by William H Ukers (1922), accessed via Project Gutenberg

- *The Illustrated Pepys* edited by Robert Latham, Penguin Books (1979)

- *London and the 17th Century* by Margarette Lincoln, Yale University Press (2021)

- *Samuel Pepys: The Unequalled Self* by Claire Tomalin, Penguin Books (2003)

- *The Time Traveller's Guide to Restoration Britain* by Ian Mortimer, Penguin Books (2017)

Printed in Dunstable, United Kingdom